The Corn Maze

Book IV

By Kaye Marie Giuliani

Text copyright @ 2016 Kaye M. Giuliani
All Rights Reserved

This book is lovingly dedicated to my father, Fred Kendall, Sr., in honor of his steadfast love and dedication to fostering creativity in me throughout my lifetime and supporting me in my every artistic endeavor.

Thanks are also due to Kathy Parr and Leonard Greenberg for their faithful assistance in the pre-reading and editing department. I couldn't have completed this book without either one of you! Thanks.

Table of Contents

Foreword	1
Call on Line Three	5
Harry Potter Theme	10
Feeling Blue	15
Matthew Gets His Wish	18
Spill on Aisle Four	23
Voicemail	27
Everything's on the Table	33
Seeing the Forest for the Trees	37
Where the F*** Am I?	41
Death on Standby	45
I'll Drive	50
Water, Water Everywhere	54
Two?	58
Baby Business	63
Arrest Him!	68
Code Blue	72
Anarchy	75

Take me to your Leader	79
I See You	83
It's Alive	95
Hit me (Baby) One More Time	103
'Trussed' in Me	108
Misty Water-Colored Memories	115
A Rose by Any Other Name	119
Throne of Chairs	122
Momma Needs a Milkshake	126
Romancing the (Portal) Stone	131
It's good to be King	134
Hear Ye! Hear Ye!	138
Murder in the High Trees	145
I'll Be There	150
Absent Without Representation	153
Dream Walking	157
Doe, a Deer	162
Brisballah and the Stone	168
A Little Help?	173
New Arrivals	176
Whitley? Alisha Lynn?	179
Matthew's Wild Ride	183
Prince Charming Awaits?	187

The Second Son	190
Then There Were Three	193
The Gingerbread House	199
Tracking Wheels	202
Daddy's Here	206
The Face of the Future	209
A Real 'Squear'	214
A Whole New Chapter	218
Voices in the Walls	221
Mission Impossible	225
Squear-eyed View	228
One Story to Go, Please	231
New Beginnings	235
A Star is Born!	238
Long Time, No See	242
Abandoned Treasures	246
The Wall of Relics	251
Where's Everybody?	255
First Contact	260
A Basket full of Squear	264
Made for Breaking	268
The Knowing	272
Look Who's Coming to Dinner	274

Pick-Up Line	277
Facing the Music	280
Love at First Sight	284
Reaching Out	290
Distracted Driver	293
Ups and Downs	296
A Voice from Beyond	301
Erlisherrr!	304
That can't be the end...Right?	306

Foreword

In The Corn Maze, Books I, II and III a young woman named Alisha Lynn Whitley takes advantage of a free Saturday afternoon to enjoy the neighborhood corn maze and disappears without explanation.

Alisha had just started her senior year in high school and was busily anticipating a lot of stressful life decisions regarding college, career and future income -- all of the anxieties that accompany the usual traumas of growing up and leaving home.

Daydreaming through the maze, however, Alisha suddenly comes to the realization that she has been walking for a very long time. The sun is going down, and she has become lost amidst the corn stalks.

Without realizing it, Alisha has rested her body against a large red boulder that opens up a portal to another reality and is unknowingly jettisoned into a life-long adventure among strange beings and hitherto unknown civilizations.

Early on, Alisha befriends a strange animal that is part squirrel and part bear (Alisha christens this creature a "squear"), whom she names, "Ahqui."

An odd pair, certainly, Alisha and Ahqui still manage to struggle through some harrowing life-and-death challenges with a great deal of skill and an eccentric flair for absurdity.

During the journey, Alisha and Ahqui meet a handsome Jurrah by the name of Rhamas. Rhamas and Alisha fall in love and are married in a dimension known as "Natalo I," but soon afterwards find themselves on the run from a wicked wizard known far and wide as the "Wise Man of Agrigar" and a band of Jurrah man-hunters in pursuit of a human criminal whom they had recently seen to be in the company of Alisha's squear.

As Book II opens, Alisha, Rhamas and Ahqui have just come through another portal only to have it instantly destroyed by a bizarre earthquake, leaving them high and dry in a place that resembles Alisha's home world of Odenton, MD.

As they sit amid the rubble of the quake, Alisha believes she overhears some people speaking "Maryland,"

(English), and she allows herself to be cautiously encouraged that home might be just around the corner, after all.

In The Corn Maze, Book III, our Hero and Heroine have survived a sea of gemstones, and a group of three-eyed Slug creatures ('Slickies'), only to be rescued by a royal barge and asked to strip naked and receive identifying tattoos on their faces.

The new city is called, "Topazial," and is comprised of a mountain of blue topaz with hundreds of cave dwellings carved into its sides. While there, the couple becomes wealthy, pregnant, and victorious over their wicked adversary, The Wise Man of the Agrigar.

Here we are now as we begin the next book in the series, "The Corn Maze, Book IV." Alisha and Rhamas have swooped through the wishing bench portal that is hidden away in John (Jack) Downs Park, Pasadena, MD and have summoned an ambulance for emergency transport to the Baltimore Washington Medical Center.

Alisha is in early labor and things aren't going well!

At the same time, Alisha's brother, Matthew, has somehow managed to get sucked into the very portal that took Alisha years before! And, to make matters worse, he has just enjoyed his first kiss with his new love, Tori Chandler, whom he may never find his way home to kiss again.

How does Alisha's father handle the news of her pregnancy and imminent delivery? Will Matthew ever be heard from again? Will Alisha's mother come up with any more creative groupings of four-letter words?

A world of suspense and adventure awaits (and, it's the one we already live in)!

Call on Line Three

"Mr. Whitley?" Grant's middle-aged administrative assistant's round face was wedged in the crack of the partially-opened conference room door, looking more florid and constipated than usual.

"Janet?"

"You have a call on line three from Baltimore Washington Medical Center. The woman says it is an emergency."

"An emergency?" Grant shot out of his chair and headed for the door. "Gentlemen, ladies, please excuse me. Frank? Take over for me."

Every step towards his office was accompanied by one thunderous beat of his heart. A thin film of perspiration was wrapping itself around his face, neck, hands and back.

Carolyn. Oh my God. Carolyn. She must have had an accident.

But, as he entered the office, collapsed into his chair and reached for the phone, he thought...

Matthew! Oh my God. Could it be Matthew?

Grant balanced the receiver between his sweat-soaked face and his shoulder – pressed the blinking number 3 and listened.

"Hello? This is Grant Whitley."

"Hello, Mr. Whitley. A young man just brought your daughter into our Emergency room."

"What?"

"Do you have a daughter named Alisha?"

Now Grant could hear his heartbeat in both ears.

"Yes. I did. I mean. Yes, I do!"

"Well, she has just gone into surgery for an emergency C-section."

"What?"

"Yes. She was unconscious and non-responsive upon arrival. The doctors are going to do their best, but they can't make any promises."

"Did you just say my daughter is having a C-section?"

"Yes sir."

"Isn't that what they do for…"

"High-risk deliveries."

"Oh. Oh. Yes, of course it is."

"Are you alright, sir?"

"Yes. Well, no but yes. I will call her mother and we will get there as soon as we can."

"That would be best, sir. Let them know who you are at the nurse's station on the fifth floor, labor and delivery. I hope everything goes well for your family."

"Yes. Fifth floor nurse's station. Labor and delivery. I'm on my way."

The receiver weighed at least ten pounds as he dropped it, gratefully, into its cradle.

Grant raised his eyes to see Janet watching him, fretfully, through the glass door.

Not knowing what else to do, he waved at Janet.

My daughter, Alisha, is in the hospital having a… She's having a… My daughter is…

Through a fog of near-stroke-level anxiety, Grant Whitley

fumbled for his cell phone and lifted his suit coat off the elegant, walnut coat tree that Carolyn had given him for Christmas.

Carolyn. Oh my God.

Pushing through the office door, the shell-shocked lawyer was suddenly bombarded with a wall of sound. The printer was printing. The phones were ringing. Janet was between him and the elevators running her mouth and making sympathetic noises that his brain could only process as "Wah wah waah wah wah."

The elevator said, "DING!" with all of the temerity of a rifle blast, and then he was inside – alone – riding down and down and down.

Grant pushed his speed dial link for Carolyn. His hands were shaking violently as he waited for her to pick up. The phone rang 10 times and went to voicemail. He hung up and tried again.

Carolyn. Where are you? Our daughter is having a…

Grant gulped nothing down a dry throat.

Alisha is having an emergency…

He reached his car in the parking garage and fumbled

with the door. Carolyn's phone rang and rang with no answer.

Baby...

At the next red light, Grant dialed his son.

C'mon, Matthew. You can't have gotten that far away. Answer your damn phone!

Harry Potter Theme

Carolyn Whitley was exhausted. The assault she had launched against the Ghama Traya (a magically-imbued red boulder) in her front yard had been appallingly ineffective. Not so much as a pebble had come free as a result of her kicking and clawing efforts. Carolyn's new shoes were destroyed, as was her manicure, her voice, and perhaps a few toes.

I think I broke some toes! Oh, ouch! Oh, Matthew, how am I going to bear losing another child to that damned rock?

It was then that Carolyn noticed the deflated and tear-stained Tori Chandler, sitting in a patch of dirt and propped up against a nearby maple tree.

"I guess I've been putting on quite a show, huh?" Carolyn asked. "Think any of the neighbors called in the men with the butterfly nets?"

Carolyn – not waiting for an answer -- dropped to the lawn in a heap.

"Nope. The lady two houses down came out on her porch, but ducked right back inside after a minute or two. I think your – um – choice of verbiage might have been a bit too much for her."

"It was bad, then."

"Got to give you credit, Mrs. Whitley, I've never heard anything quite like it."

"Yeah. Well. Sorry about that, but under the circumstances…"

"It's okay. You were just saying what I was feeling."

"What are we going to do, Tori? How are we going to get him back?"

For the 15th time the Harry Potter theme could be heard tinkling out of Carolyn's discarded cell phone. The two women seemed to take notice, but nobody moved to answer it.

"What am I going to tell Mr. Whitley?" groaned Carolyn. "This will kill him, and it's all my fault."

"No, it isn't your fault. Matt and I have been trying to

get through that portal all day – with no success."

"You've what?" Carolyn was incredulous.

"Matthew couldn't get past his need to see the things Alisha saw. He has wanted to follow her ever since he found her journal."

"Why would the two of you do something like that to your families? You were just going to zap off together without leaving so much as a note behind? Matthew has seen the kind of suffering that can cause. I can't believe he would be so selfish."

Tori heaved a sigh and dropped her head into her hands.

"Mrs. Whitley, I don't know what we were thinking. Somehow, I didn't believe some mystical portal was going to open up and suck us in. Even though I was pretty sure that rock had been the one that had taken Alisha. The experiment had seemed like more of a game at the time. I am very sorry."

"Well, he hadn't passed through until I showed up screaming like a banshee and knocking him off balance."

"Nobody's fault, it just happened," Tori said. "Besides, it was what Matthew wanted."

"What Matthew wanted? That's rich. What about me? What about what I wanted? Maybe I want to whoosh out of this mess and find a less screwed-up existence. What about his physical therapy? How is he going to get around out there in 'Neverland' without legs? Doesn't anybody think things through to their natural conclusion?"

The Harry Potter theme interrupted and caused both sets of eyes to track and focus on the lonely cell phone, currently perched face up, on a clump of grass several feet away.

The screen was lit.

"That will be Grant," Carolyn croaked.

"Might be," Tori mumbled from somewhere under her hands.

"I wonder why he keeps calling? If my husband had any idea what just happened here, he'd forget my number and jump a plane to Bali."

"Sounds like a plan," agreed Tori, lifting her face to rest the back of her head against the trunk of the maple.

The ringtone played itself out to the accompaniment of a random breeze that crossed the yard and cooled the sweat on their foreheads before the display went dark.

"Maybe this is the way of the future, you know?" Tori ventured. "Soon, everybody will be stepping through portals and vacationing in exotic lands. Alisha and Matthew are just ahead of their time."

"Alisha did say that she had come across some kind of portal guidebook. Do you think she could pop back here one day and go looking for him?"

"Mrs. Whitley, I feel perfectly justified in saying that anything can happen," Tori met Carolyn's eyes and the two women shared a half-hearted smile.

The Harry Potter theme rang out again.

"Aren't you going to get that?"

"Yeah. Sure. I might as well," said Carolyn Whitley, not moving an inch.

The phone went silent.

The screen went dark.

Feeling Blue

Rhamas had never felt so afraid, confused or out of place. One person after another had come forward asking for the information Alisha had scribbled on the back of the paper that had covered their peanut butter jar. He tried to explain where they had come from and what was wrong, but all he got for that was a lot of raised eyebrows and funny looks.

"My wife is very sick trying to have our child. She asked me to bring her to this place because it has people who can save her. Is that true? Can you save them both? Where have you taken her? Can you please take me to be with her? My wife is very sick and she needs me."

The first lady, a short, fat, blue-haired woman by the name of "Martha Winetraub," wanted to know many things. She wanted to know if Rhamas had something called "health insurance," and also what the "group number" was. Mrs. Winetraub was growing impatient with all of her questions, and became brittle when asking to see something called "identification," or his "driver's license."

Rhamas had no idea what those things were, so he just kept showing them the piece of paper that Alisha had given him. He kept pointing out that it had words and numbers on it, but then there were the funny looks again.

Finally, a lady dressed in blue paper with a funny blue hat and matching shoes led him into an empty hallway and handed him some paper clothes of his own.

"Scrub up and put these on," she instructed in a brusque, take-no-prisoners voice.

Rhamas tried to appear knowledgeable. "I will scrub up and put these on," he repeated.

The blue-paper lady looked Rhamas up and down for a minute, then led him to a sink and showed Rhamas how to wash his hands clear up to his elbows and rinse them off under the water.

"Is this your first?" The lady asked.

"First?"

The lady shook her head and rolled her eyes. "Now, put these on right over your clothes."

It had seemed like a ridiculous thing to do, but

Rhamas didn't want to make this woman angry. He needed to be with Alisha, and he was determined to do whatever was asked of him – no matter how bizarre it might seem.

Once outfitted in the blue paper clothes, Rhamas followed the woman through two doors that opened when she pushed a large square on the wall.

Things happened every second that made him want to stop and investigate, but he had learned a long time ago to act bored when magic doors opened and little people moved inside glass-covered boxes, etc. If you got all excited over everything, the people would think you were stupid.

The next thing he saw was very upsetting. Alisha was on a table surrounded by paper people with masks on their faces. She was under a blue paper tent from her waist down, and Rhamas could see a table with knives and tools lined up on it.

There were lights flashing and beeping sounds. There was a television with two crooked lines moving across it. The room smelled funny and everything started to tip to one side... Rhamas felt like he was going to faint.

Matthew Gets His Wish

The last clear memory that Matthew Whitley has is of hearing his mother yelling "Get away from that goddamned rock!" He knows now that he must have managed, accidentally, to achieve the correct hand position to open Ghama Traya's portal, and that he has left his front yard for parts unknown.

Where was I sitting when it happened? Matthew asked himself, sizing up the boulder and the relative geography so that he would have a better idea of how to open it again when he was ready to return.

Because, I'm not ready to return. He thought, flushing with a combination of exhilaration and fear. *I just got here!*

Matthew could see a vast forest off in the distance to his right, and immediately recognized it as the place where Alisha had spent her first months in Natalo I (or WTFAI, as Alisha called it).

I was sitting on the top of the rock, having just

kissed Tori (Wow! I kissed Tori!). Or, did she kiss me? When my mother's voice startled me, I must have fallen backwards a bit and caught myself with both hands.... Here and here?

Matthew made a mental note, but was careful not to touch the stone again. Instead he scanned the barren field between his current position and the imposing forest. He wondered what Alisha must have felt, seeing it off in the distance – a hulk of mysterious darkness – waiting to consume her. The trees were huge, even from a great distance. And, it was a great distance.

It would be a healthy hike. Still, Matthew felt he simply had to find his sister's shelter (if anything was left of it) and the little stream that had sustained her during what must have been a terrifying ordeal.

I have the advantage. I know where I am, and that nothing lives here. I also know that the Ghama Traya will open a door to Natalo II, where the Agrigars live.

Then Matthew had a very disturbing realization. There was no corn. Alisha had survived on corn that she had routinely gathered out of this cornfield.

When is the corn planted? Ummm. Somewhere

around July? August? Mathew didn't know. Clearly, the planting had not yet occurred.

Maybe that is a good thing? I will show myself to the Agrigars when they come to do their planting, and they will take me with them to Natalo II.

The Agrigars were afraid of Alisha, at first, but became friends shortly thereafter. Surely they would welcome him with open arms, too. He was Alisha's brother, after all. Then, everything would be good.

I would have plenty to eat, and a place to stay, and friends... He mused.

For a fleeting moment, Matthew thought about Tori and his mother, and how worried they must be. His eyes fixed on the Ghama Traya with thoughts of heading home first and exploring later, but...

I'm here! This is another dimension, and I'm actually here! It is real and amazing and exciting and...

Still, Matthew knew that a decision to stay and explore this new dimension would send a message to Tori that he didn't want her to receive; "I made it through and decided to go ahead without you."

How would you feel if it had been Tori who had been

the first to make it through the portal? he thought, feeling small.

Matthew knew that he wasn't prepared for any kind of survival challenge. No food or water. No extra clothing or blankets. (For that matter, he could have brought the family tent along and camped in style and comfort).

I'm just going to look around for a while, first. Then, I'll go back. It won't take long to get to the trees, will it? A few hours, maybe? I could always tell them it took me that long to figure out how to get back...

Knowing that powering his chair was going to be an issue in the near future; Matthew disengaged the automatic drivers and pushed his chair manually towards the forest. It was rough and dusty going.

The field was far from smooth, prickly with the stubs of last year's corn stalks and parched from lack of rainfall.

Matthew's chair stirred up an impressive cloud as it bumped and skidded along the arid terrain. The dust found its way into his nostrils and filled his mouth with grit that was difficult to spit out from his dry throat.

An hour passed, and the forest didn't seem to be getting any closer. Matthew's thirst was becoming unbearable, and he stopped to look back at the portal. He found himself wishing that he had just gone home and come back later, more prepared.

There is water in the forest. Matthew told himself. *Alisha found a stream and so will I.* But, he didn't know how far inside the forest he would have to go, or even which direction to travel in order to find water. The number of things he didn't know was outnumbering the things he did, and Matthew was very, very thirsty.

Maybe I should go back home and get some supplies together before I go any further? Matthew thought, but, as he looked back over his shoulder at the distance he had already travelled, he knew that his only choice was to continue on his chosen path and hope that he was as lucky as Alisha had been in finding water and a safe place to shelter for the night.

Spill on Aisle Four

Grant Whitley loosened his tie and unbuttoned the top button of his starched white shirt. His suit jacket had been tossed into the back seat of the Cadillac SUV, and was currently acquiring creases where creases shouldn't be, but Grant didn't care.

As a successful attorney and a card-carrying obsessive compulsive, Grant had always preferred suit jackets without any unsightly wrinkly bits. He was tall, well-built, and always right – about everything.

The Emergency parking had been packed, and it had taken forever to find a spot on the farthest outer reaches of the lot. Grant had parked, locked the shiny Black Escalade, patted his back pocket to make sure he had his wallet, and started hoofing it towards the hospital's Emergency Room entrance.

Alisha was in trouble. Real trouble. *That kind* of trouble. Mr. Whitley decided that his first order of business was to find the young man that brought her into the emergency room and share with him a large and loud piece of his mind.

No. My first stop is the maternity ward nurse's station to find out how she's doing. If the, um, birth had taken place. If my daughter is still alive.

There was strange buzzing sound in his ears, and Grant became aware that he was sweating profusely.

I don't feel right, he thought. *I think I'm going to have a heart attack.*

The thought made him laugh.

If I'm going to collapse, this is probably the best place to do it.

His levity was short-lived, however, as the buzzing sound began to swell and Grant noticed things going all dark and foggy behind his eyes.

Hold up, sport. Get some air. Everything's going to be okay.

Grant leaned against the rear of a Prius. He swept a lock of sodden hair off his forehead. He just needed to calm down.

It would all be a lot better if Carolyn had just answered her phone. Where could she be?

Maybe she got a call from the hospital, too? That's it! Grant allowed himself to relax a bit.

She's probably already inside waiting for me. I'll bet she had to turn her phone off in the waiting room. I wonder how she's taking the news? She always dreamed of having a...

A flush of stomach acids rose up in Grant's throat and his chest burned.

Alisha is probably already in surgery. There's nothing I can do. No need to rush. There's certainly no reason to kill myself getting there.

Almost as soon as he had finished that thought, Grant Whitley, successful lawyer, devoted husband and father of two (most of the time) keeled over onto the pavement with an accompanying "CRUNCH!" sound as his face planted itself on the first available surface without taking into consideration the general health and well-being of his nose.

That was a sound that had the power to make people wince for a city block -- human face, flattening itself on black pavement. Mr. Whitley wasn't in any pain, however. In fact, Grant Whitley's heart was taking a much-needed 'time out.'

He wasn't bothered when a crowd of strangers started to gather around and holler at him. Didn't mind when some strange man jostled him roughly, rolled him over and planted a lingering kiss on his lips.

Really, when you think about it, those things could be rather worrying in any other state of mind.

The one good thing to come of all of it was that Grant Whitley, Esq. was swiftly loaded onto a gurney and given a ride the rest of the way.

Problem solved.

Voicemail

Tori helped Mrs. Whitley to her feet and guided her towards the house, picking up stray items along the way. The cell phone had gone curiously silent over the past several minutes, but was soon rescued along with other items that had exploded from the mysterious depths of Carolyn's purse as she had hurried to exact her vengeance on the Ghama Traya.

"I think I'm okay to go the rest of the way on my own," Carolyn said. "Thanks for picking everything up. I just... I just..."

That was when the floodgates opened up once again, and Mrs. Whitley collapsed against the diminutive cheer leader along with a veritable tsunami of tears.

"Oh, we'll get him back, Mrs. Whitley. Don't worry, okay? At least we know where he went and how he got there. If Alisha doesn't come home soon, I'll go and find

Matthew myself."

"You will?" Carolyn sniffed.

"Of course, I will! We were supposed to go on that adventure together, you know? Your son kind-of left me holding the bag – no pun intended."

A tentative smile broke out on Mrs. Whitley's face.

"I suppose it is different this time around. When Alisha disappeared…"

"Right. When Alisha took off missing, you had no idea what could have happened to her. It could have been a sex freak or a serial killer or just about any horrible thing. This time we know what Matthew's gone and done, don't we? We'll get him back before you know it. Matter of fact, I'm surprised he hasn't come back on his own, already."

"It should be easy, shouldn't it? Doesn't he just have to touch the rock again in the same places to get back?"

"That's what Alisha said in her journal, so I'm sure that's all there is to it."

"We can follow him, if we can just figure out where his hands were when he zapped out of sight!" Carolyn whirled about and headed back towards the Ghama Traya before Tori could grab hold properly.

"Whoa! Let's go inside and have some iced tea or something and figure out what we're going to do this time around. I don't think having everyone going off half-cocked and willy-nilly all over the place is going to solve anything."

"No, I guess you're right," Carolyn sniffed and allowed herself to be steered onto the front porch.

"Where are your keys?" Tori asked patiently, offering the overstuffed handbag to Mrs. Whitley.

"They are in here somewhere," said Carolyn, digging furiously through the cosmetic carnage and balled-up receipts and coming up empty time and time again.

"Ah! Here they are," Mrs. Whitley dropped the bundle of keys into Tori's upturned palm and waited for the house to be unlocked so that she could find a place crumple.

Tori opened the door and settled Mrs. Whitley onto the sofa before heading for the kitchen to find something cool to drink.

"What would you like to have, Mrs. Whitley? Water? Milk? Diet Coke? Sprite?"

"Diet Coke, please."

"Where do you keep your glasses?" Tori opened

and closed cabinet doors.

"No glass for me, Tori. I'm fine with the can."

"Cool." Tori kicked off her sneakers and padded into the living room with two cans of Diet Coke and handed one to Mrs. Whitley before slipping gratefully into the sofa's matching chair-and-a-half.

"You should probably try to call your husband," Tori said, after two particularly satisfying gulps of cold soda.

"Oh, lord. What am I going to tell him?"

"I'd just start with finding out why he was calling you, and then take it one word at a time."

"Yes. I guess that would be best, wouldn't it?"

"Are you sure it was your husband who was trying to reach you?"

"Pretty sure. Nobody ever calls me except Grant and Matthew and... well..."

"Gotcha," replied Tori, hoping to avoid another crying jag.

Carolyn dialed and held the phone to her ear. After a moment she made a face and tried again. "He isn't picking up," she said.

"That isn't like him. He always takes my calls."

"Did he leave any voicemails?"

"Oh gee," she exclaimed after a brief examination of her screen. "There are seven messages! Seven!"

"Sounds like you've got some listening to do. Mind if I make a sandwich?"

Carolyn waved Tori onward and started going through the voicemails.

"Carolyn? Please call me back as soon as you get this message. It's important."

The refrigerator door opened and closed and a plastic bag rustled.

"I'm making a ham and cheese. Do you want me to make one for you?" Tori called out from the kitchen.

"Sure! Thanks. That sounds good."

"Carolyn? Where are you? This is an emergency, honey. Please call me right back, okay?"

"No problem. Mustard or mayo?"

"Mustard."

"Carolyn! I need you! What the hell is going on over there? Call me!"

Tori came back with the sandwiches and settled back into her spot.

"Anything yet?"

Carolyn shrugged her shoulders. "My husband has left three messages asking me to call him."

"Oh." Tori tucked into the ham and cheese on potato bread with mayo. It was heavenly. Apparently, interdimensional travel catastrophes worked up an appetite.

"Hello. This is a message for Carolyn Whitley. I am calling from Baltimore Washington Medical Center. A young man has given me your number as contact information for a patient that has just come into our emergency room. Please call me back at…"

Carolyn Whitley's eyes opened wide and she stood up, dumping ham and cheese with mustard all over herself, her sofa and the linen-colored carpeting.

"I've got to go! Grant's been taken to the hospital!"

Everything's on the Table

A nurse locked the wheels on Alisha's gurney and two more helped to transfer her to the operating table. The whole thing might have been scary for another girl, but to Alisha, it was a profound relief.

I'm safe now. Finally. I am surrounded by real doctors who are going to take the baby out of me and do their best to save our lives. I am so tired. I just want to sleep.

Alisha closed her eyes and thought about what it was going to be like to hold her own infant. A boy, or a girl. Whatever, it really didn't matter. *Where is Rhamas? Are they going to let him be here for the birth?*

"Excuse me, Nurse? Where is my husband? Is he going to be here with me?"

"Yes, hon. He is getting scrubbed up while we get everything prepared for surgery. It will only be a few more minutes. How are you doing?"

The nurse was built as any competent surgical nurse should be, large-breasted and round-bodied – the comforting sort. She wore an I.D. tag, but it was turned around and impossible to read.

"I am fine. Relieved. I just want it to be over."

The nurse exchanged a worried glance with the doctor.

Alisha knew they were concerned about her chances of coming through the surgery alive, but she was too tired to feel any anxiety at the prospect. Rhamas would be with her soon, and they would see their baby. Besides, Alisha was sure that she would get better as soon as the child was out of her body.

A blue drape was being set up between her face and her abdomen. Alisha had seen Cesarean sections performed on television from every possible angle, so none of this was a surprise. A catheter had been inserted to collect her urine during surgery, monitoring leads had been attached to track her vital signs, she had been shaved and wiped with antiseptic wash, the anesthesia was on board and being carefully watched.

Where is Rhamas? What is taking him so long?

Alisha felt awful. From one minute to the next she wasn't sure that she could remain conscious. Her head ached horribly, and she wanted to vomit even though she hadn't eaten anything substantial for days.

"Okay, Miss Alisha," the squishy nurse said, laying a comforting hand on her shoulder. "I'll just go and get that man of yours so we can get this show on the road."

"Yes, please," Alisha whispered. Things beeped and whirred all around her, but time didn't pass the way it should have. Alisha looked at the blue curtain between her and her abdomen and waited for Rhamas.

All that she needed now was to see his face. As soon as that happened, Alisha would be able to relax and pass everything onto her husband's broad shoulders. No matter who lived or died from that point onward, Rhamas would see it through. He was her rock.

"Are my parents here?" Alisha asked the room.

"I'm sure if they're not here, yet, they are on their way," the masked and gloved doctor said. "You can ask nurse Hamsby when she comes back."

The thought of her parents changed the pulse rate

that beeped so loudly from somewhere nearby. This wasn't exactly the way Alisha had planned to introduce her husband and baby to her family.

Just as that train of thought was about to become overwhelming, nurse Hamsby pushed through the operating room doors with Rhamas in tow.

"Rhamas," Alisha smiled with obvious relief. "You're here, and now everything is going to be okay."

"I am with you, sweet one," he murmured in Jurrah. "You and the child are safe in my heart."

Seeing the Forest for the Trees

The sun went down and the forest was plunged into darkness. Matthew's chair got caught up on every root and shrub, and the effort of working it free over and over again was exhausting. At some point, he reached a clearing and stopped to catch his breath.

I should dump this thing and move forward with my arms, alone. Matthew thought, knowing that he'd be able to cover more ground that way. *I could always come back for it after I've found water.*

In the end, he had abandoned the chair. It had been much faster to move through the forest without it, just as Matthew had predicted. Still, it was worrisome to leave it behind. He decided that he should begin to mark his path from that point onward, so that there would be no problem finding the chair again later.

Matthew found a sharp-ish rock and began to

scratch markings into the bark of the trees that he passed. That endeavor slowed him down a bit, but was necessary. Getting lost in that forest was not something Matthew wanted to contemplate. The trees were huge! They towered so far above him that any hope of climbing into the branches to sleep was dashed. At least the weather was clear, and he wasn't freezing the way his sister had been come nightfall in this desolate place.

The need for water had gone from theory to the harshest of realities at this point. It had been hours since he'd left Maryland, and even longer since he'd had anything to drink. Matthew was beginning to grasp the enormity of his dilemma. His respect for Alisha was growing by the minute.

Are we having fun, yet?

This adventure stuff wasn't all that it was cracked up to be. He was tired, hungry, thirsty, dirty and miserable – and he'd just barely arrived!

I'll find the stream, spend the night, and head back first thing in the morning. Matthew assured himself.

The next time I venture into this dimension, I'll come prepared with water (water, water, water), and all of the camping gear I can carry – and Tori.

Matthew replayed Tori's kiss in his mind as he fought his way forward through the creepy forest. Her mouth had been so soft and willing. She had opened her eyes as their lips parted, and they were as warm and smiling as ever he had seen them. God, but she was beautiful.

Leave it to his mother to screw such a stellar moment up so royally.

Thanks, Mom. From time to time, Matthew would stop to listen for the sound of water.

The silence when he did so was so complete that his heart was struck with a profound sense of loneliness and loss. There were no crickets, gnats, mosquitos, squirrels, bats, or birds. Matthew assumed that a good breeze would cause the leaves in the canopy above to rustle reassuringly, but there was no breeze tonight. Everything was as still as the grave.

Okay, I've had enough adventure. I'm ready for a burger, fries and coke in front of the latest episode of "How Things Work." Somehow, just knowing that those things still existed somewhere was heartening to Matthew.

I'll go home tomorrow afternoon – evening, at the latest. Mom will be torn up, but over the moon to see me. Tori will be relieved and probably want to kiss me again, first thing. Dad? Well, best not to think about how Dad will greet me. He gets so uptight about everything.

A sound came to Matthew's ears that swept every worry from his mind. It sounded like water. He smelled the air and thought that he could even smell the water. Matthew smiled and cracked the skin on his chapped lower lip. He touched it, gingerly, and his finger came away with a tiny spot of blood on it.

Ouch. That sucks.

Where the F*** Am I?

"Mr. Whitley? Mr. Whitley? Can you hear me?"

"I think he is coming around."

"Have you been able to locate any family members?"

"Not yet. His business card has an office number, should I call that?"

"There's nothing on his cell?"

"Not anything I can use -- just first names. Carolyn, Becky, Fred: Could be anybody."

"Okay. Let's wait for him to regain consciousness, then."

"His vital signs are improving. BP is 134/87. Heart rate is normal. Oxygen levels hovering around 93%."

Grant could hear people discussing him somewhere off in the distance. He wanted to tell the voices to call his wife, but he couldn't remember her name at the moment, or open his eyes. There was something covering his mouth and nose, at any rate, so he just laid there.

Where the fuck am I?

Grant Whitley needed his rest. Things were stressful right now, he knew, but he couldn't remember the cause of his anxiety. It would come to him, eventually. Hadn't the voices just said he was getting better?

I think that I am in the hospital. Yes. I'm certain of it. That is good. I was trying to get to the hospital, wasn't I? And, I'm here. Job well done. It just bothers me a bit that I can't remember having arrived...

"Mr. Whitley? Mr. Whitley? Can you hear me? If you can hear me, please squeeze my hand."

Can I squeeze his hand? I may be able to do that. Am I holding his hand? No, I don't think so... Wait! There it is. Okay, one, two, three and s-q-u-e-e-z-e. "Okay. We've got him," said the ER doc.

"Mr. Whitley, you have had a heart attack, actually, what we call a Myocardial Infarction. You collapsed in the hospital parking lot and were given CPR right away by a Good Samaritan. He saved your life! We are admitting you to our ICU for observation. Do you understand?"

A heart attack? The man must be delusional. I am in excellent shape for a man my age. Grant thought. *Wait. How old am I?*

Grant nodded and squeezed the hand again.

This is an upsetting development, but also a relief. I need someone to bring me juice and pudding on a tray. Some morphine wouldn't go amiss, either. I am under a great deal of stress, after all – even if I can't remember what it is I'm finding so stressful...

"Someone will be here, shortly, to take you to your room. Mr. Whitley? Is there anybody you would like us to notify? Perhaps a number on your cell?"

Yes! Of course there is somebody you should notify! What do you think that I'm a lonely homeless person? I think not! I am a hard-hitting, top-notch trial attorney, for cripe's sake!

But he couldn't make his mouth work properly, so all he said was, "All Arrow In."

"You want me to call Carolyn? Is that your wife?"

Grant nodded, gratefully. Thank heavens for people who could translate the language of MI (Myocardial

Infarction).

Grant had been too exhausted from his first attempt at speech to even imagine having to repeat himself.

"Okay, Mr. Whitley. The nurse will call your wife. Someone will be here in a few minutes to take you to your room."

You said that, already. I'm disabled, not stupid. Grant thought, feeling annoyed all over again.

Death on Standby

Rhamas leaned in to kiss Alisha on the forehead. He brushed the hair away from her face, and felt the clammy coolness of the freshly dead.

She has Death in her eyes. Rhamas thought with a shudder. *He is waiting to take her away from me, and the acceptance of this is already living within her heart.*

"You are safe in the good hospital now, my love," Rhamas coaxed in his native language. "These people in the paper shirts and masks are going to save you. I believe this! Now, you must believe this. We have made the dangerous journey, our child is ready to join us. You have done well! How strong you have been! Please stay strong for only a moment more? I beg you to have faith in our lives together. Yes. I see Death. I know his voice is strong in you. Please do not forget the strength of your husband! My arms are like iron, and my love for you is great. Trust that I will pull you free of Death's cold grasp, my love, my wife."

A single tear formed in Alisha's eye, quivered there for a moment, then dropped from her dark lashes onto her cheek.

Alisha met his gaze and nodded. "I'll try." She whispered. "I know you are the stronger one."

The surgical team had continued to ready themselves while the couple exchanged words in an unknown language. When the husband had stopped talking and looked up at him, the surgeon took over.

"We are ready to begin," the surgeon's eyes smiled encouragingly over his moving mask. "Alisha? Do you feel anything when I touch you here?"

"No. Nothing."

"Good. Okay, I am going to make the first incision. This will create an opening in your abdominal wall. The second step will be to access your uterus, and then we will get to see your baby! Are you ready? All you will feel is a little pressure."

Rhamas was standing at Alisha's head where his eyes were shielded from the horror of what was happening to her. The smell of blood mixed with other odors in the room and he began to feel lightheaded.

"Are you okay over there, Dad? Susan, keep your eye on him, okay? He looks a little shaky."

"I am not this shaky that you say. I am a Jurrah warrior. I am worried only for my wife," Rhamas said, throwing out his chest and getting control of his breathing. "Oh. Okay. Good," the surgeon said. "It won't be long now. I am opening up the uterine wall, Alisha. I see your baby! Now, let me get my hands around and bring it…"

There was an uncomfortable silence. Alisha raised her head from the pillow, Rhamas leaned forward to see what was happening.

"And, you have a healthy baby girl!"

A tiny red face made its appearance over the edge of the paper barrier, followed by an equally tiny and equally red body, legs and feet.

"Oh, Rhamas! Look at her! Our baby! She is the most beautiful thing I have ever seen."

Rhamas kissed his wife on the mouth and nodded. He was too full of emotion to say a word. There were hot tears running down his cheeks and he was unable to speak for the love that he felt for this precious little person.

"Do you want to cut the cord, Dad?"

Rhamas shook his head. He wasn't planning to cut anything. The surgeon did the honors and the freshly clamped infant was handed off to the pediatric team for evaluation.

"Okay, Alisha. We aren't quite done yet. Let's let the nurses get her cleaned up and weighed while we get you all put back together. Are you feeling any pain?"

"No, but I am getting very dizzy."

There was a change in the doctor's expression and he was suddenly all business.

"Susan, Becky, please take Daddy and Baby to the nursery to fill out some paperwork."

"I will stay." Rhamas puffed out his impressive muscles and planted his feet firmly on the shiny linoleum.

"Of course you want to stay, Mr. Whitley, but somebody has to go with the baby to the nursery, and your wife is certainly not able to do it. Now, come along, and congratulations! You have a beautiful new daughter! You must be so proud."

Rhamas couldn't help but respond to the maternal warmth of nurse Hamsby, so he spared one worried glance at his wife and one warning glare at the surgeon before allowing himself to be ushered off to another, equally confusing, location somewhere within the hospital.

"She's hemorrhaging!" the surgeon announced between clenched teeth as soon as the doors had closed behind Rhamas and Nurse Hamsby. "Start a pint of A+, Stat!"

"Patient is going into arrest, doctor."

"Send out a Code Blue!"

Alisha was vaguely aware of the commotion going on all around her, but her awareness was fractured by a feeling of lightness. Her body wasn't heavy anymore. She felt as though she could almost step out of it and float away.

I will leave this mess for the doctors to contend with, Alisha thought. *I want to go with Rhamas and the baby right now. I'll come back later when the surgeons are finished. I wonder what we will name our little princess?*

I'll Drive

Tori scooped up Mrs. Whitley's keys from the coffee table and ran to collect her sneakers.

"Oh my God! Which hospital?"

"Baltimore Washington Medical Center."

"Okay. Come on. I'll drive."

"But, I have mustard all down the front of me…"

"Not a problem. Everybody in the emergency room looks awful. It's a 'thing'. Come on! We have to get going!"

"The person who called never said what was wrong with him, only that some young man had brought in a family member and it was an emergency."

"No worries. We are only ten minutes away. We'll find out everything once we get there."

"Why didn't Grant just tell me he was feeling bad when he left all of those messages? I would have driven him to the hospital, myself."

"That's just how men do things. They like the mystery of it all – adds to the dramatic impact. Besides, we are on our way, right? Just hang on to your hat and take a few deep breaths. We don't need for you to stroke out, right? I'd say we've had enough excitement for one day."

"What on earth could have happened?" Carolyn Whitley clutched her purse as though it was a life preserver and she was floating alone in the Indian Ocean.

"Whatever it is, we'll be there soon. Now, stop worrying and breathe!"

Tori Chandler was running on pure adrenaline.

Could this day get any worse? She thought. *This car is amazing. Two-tone leather seats, four-wheel drive, whatever kind of suspension that made you feel as though you were flying above the pavement rather than bumping along on it. I wonder what kind it is…*

Tori's eyes scanned the dash and the steering wheel for logos. *Oh. Well. Sure. It would be a Lexus. Criminy! What would it be like to have that kind of money at your disposal?*

"Ha. I'm not holding my breath."

"What?"

Tori hadn't meant to say that out loud. "Nothing. I was just having a conversation with myself."

"Oh," Mrs. Whitley sighed. "I do that. Sometimes I think I'm the only one who listens to me."

"Here's our exit. I'll drop you off at the entrance and find a parking spot, okay?"

"Yes. Thank you. That would probably be best."

"I'll call your cell so that you have my number, in case we get separated. Since the HIPAA laws went into effect, nobody can tell anybody anything about anything."

"So true. You can tell them you are his daughter, Alisha. They are much more forthcoming with family members, and there isn't much chance of the real Alisha showing up here."

"Good idea," Tori agreed. "Okay. Here you are. I'll find you, eventually. I hope Mr. Whitley is going to be alright."

"Thanks, dear," Carolyn said, hesitating to exit the car. "Whatever happens, this probably isn't the best time to tell him about Matthew."

"My lips are sealed," Tori agreed. "Now, go. Everything will be okay. I'm sure of it."

Mrs. Whitley shouldered her bag and climbed out of the car. She was afraid. There was something in her gut that told her everything was NOT going to be okay.

Not okay at all.

Water, Water Everywhere

Matthew followed the sounds of running water to a narrow stream. Contrary to all outdoor survival experts the world over, he dropped to his knees and scooped up large mouthfuls of the cool, delicious, (unsanitary and perhaps dangerous) water.

As soon as he had satisfied his burning thirst, Matthew threw off his clothes and pulled himself into the stream to bathe. His hands were covered in cuts and abrasions.

His arms ached with the effort of crawling on his hands and knees for over an hour across rough terrain. Matthew sat in the shallows and ran his hands over his knees and the stumps that extended beneath them.

The night sky was a riot of the brightest stars he had ever seen. It was like being in an old western movie, or how the sky might have looked before the dinosaurs showed up. Matthew would have to remember to tell Tori all about it. So beautiful.

Matthew had been really tall – around six foot seven

before right around feeding time on Waikiki. Being double amputated below the knees had changed his stature, considerably.

It would have been easy for Matthew to get depressed over such a setback, but he had considered the alternatives (e.g., becoming shark poop), and decided to make the best of it.

Good things had happened as a result of his injury; the auto repair garage his parents had set up for him; the cool new house and electric wheelchair with all the bells and whistles; oh, and let's not forget the lovely Tori Chandler.

Tori might have had more to do with his sister's "Mad Mystery Tour" than his shark attack, but everything had come together so nicely.

Maybe, the fully-legged Matthew would have been too afraid to talk to a knockout like Tori?

I hope Tori's not pissed off at me for leaving her behind. She must know my abrupt 'exit' was unintentional. I bet Mom is crying her eyes out and asking for a refill on her valium, though. I should have gone straight home. That would have been the right thing to do.

"No problem! I'll be back home by tomorrow night, treat everybody to a double-pepperoni with extra cheese, and we'll all have a good laugh," he said aloud to not-a-living-soul-anywhere-to-be-seen.

"All of this quietude is kind-of creepy," Matthew splashed water on his face and hair.

"Hello! Hello! Anybody out there?" His words fell flat onto the gently moving surface of the water while Matthew waited for a response that he hoped wouldn't come, and shuddered.

He was getting hungry enough to eat a bug, but there weren't any.

I am going home tomorrow. I'll fill up on pizza. Jeez, you'd think one missed meal was gonna' kill a guy.

Matthew had never been a Boy Scout, but he had gone camping with his father a few times. He figured he could get a fire started, if he really wanted to. He could rig a shelter, too, but sitting here in the gentle stream, he wasn't sure that a one-night stay was going to be worth the trouble.

I wonder what time it is? I am as underpowered as the transmission on Bruce's Ford Escort. Matthew thought.

My gears are stripped and my engine's whining.

After a few more minutes of rest, Matthew hauled his body out to air-dry on the thin strip of sand. It was a bit chillier than it had been. The temperature must be closer to 68 degrees than the 75 or 80 it had been upon his arrival at the portal.

All things considered, Matthew opted for curling up under a tree – no shelter – no fire. He was 'roughing' it.

Two?

Carolyn stepped out of her pearly Lexus as Tori drove away to park.

A young family was just leaving through the emergency department's glass doors with their son on crutches as Mrs. Whitley approached. As they passed, Carolyn smiled a sympathetic greeting, pulled her way through the first set of doors, then yanked open the right side of the second set and walked into the freshly re-vamped waiting room to join a short line of the walking wounded.

Carolyn found the modern furnishings and the blue / tan color scheme attractive and uplifting. Someone had done their homework. The recessed lighting and teak-look-alike end tables gave off the ambience of a high-priced hotel lobby, rather than a prison cafeteria. A quick evaluation of the occupants was proof that ambience wasn't making the wait any more pleasant.

The middle-aged woman with the wispy grey hair

that was staffing the triage desk seemed friendly enough and even efficient. A big improvement over the way things were the night she had brought an 11-year-old Alisha in with abdominal pains at 10:00 pm on a school night.

They had been told to go sit down and had ended up waiting for three hours, only to find out that Alisha's appendix had ruptured while they were sitting there.

"Can I help you?" the woman with the "Marjorie" nametag asked.

"Yes. I hope so," Carolyn put a death grip on the imitation bamboo handles of her purse. "I received a phone message from someone here saying that my family member had been brought in?"

"Last Name?"

"Whitley."

"Hmm. We have two Whitley's tonight. First name?"

"Grant."

"Let me see. Yes. Mr. Whitley has been admitted to our ICU. You can find him on the first floor in room 112."

"Intensive care? Do you know what he is there for?"

"No ma'am, but we just changed shifts. I'm sure

they'll be more helpful at the nurses' station."

"Thank you."

Someone tapped Carolyn on the shoulder and she jumped with a start.

"Just me."

Tori was standing there with a question mark for a face.

"They've admitted him," Carolyn said, holding back tears. "He's been taken to Intensive Care."

"Why? What happened to him? Could he have had a stroke?"

Carolyn shook her head. "I really doubt it. He is so healthy, and still pretty young in his 50's."

"C'mon," Tori took Mrs. Whitley's elbow. "We won't know anything until we get to ICU. Which floor is it on?"

"First floor. Room 112."

"When my grandfather was in the ICU, only family visitors were allowed."

"I need you to stay with me Tori, if you wouldn't mind?"

"I'd be happy to, but…"

"Just tell them you are his daughter, Alisha."

"Will do. Um, Mrs. Whitley?"

"Yes, Tori?"

"You might want to, um, run a comb through your hair, or something."

Suddenly self-conscious, Carolyn rifled through her purse for a compact, found one, and surveyed the damage. Her stylish bob had stepped outside the lines in every direction.

"Oh my. Yep. Thanks."

An elevator was already unloading two doctors and a nurse when Tori and Carolyn reached the section, so they waited for an attractive young black couple to enter before climbing on and pressing their floor.

"Interesting thing…" Carolyn mentioned casually.

"Yeah?"

"The woman in the emergency room said that they had two Whitleys come through there today."

"Pretty common name, isn't it?"

"I guess so. Still, a bit odd, wouldn't you say?"

Tori shrugged.

"Think about it, Tori. It's probably safe to say that the emergency room is dealing with fewer than 100 people..."

"Could be more, but, okay."

"So, what are the odds that there would be two people with the same last name coming through emergency in the same hospital on the same day at around the same time?"

"Pretty big coincidence, I guess."

"Yep. See what I mean? Just odd."

Baby Business

Rhamas followed the blue-paper-lady and his new daughter down a long hall and to the right. He wondered why the lady wasn't letting him carry his own infant, rather than wheeling her down the hallway in a cart.

Imagine his surprise when they reached the nursery! There must have been a dozen babies in carts, all lined up in rows. Rhamas had never seen so many infants in one place at the same time. He rotated a complete 360 degree turn and didn't see a single mother, either. Not one!

"Where are all of their mothers?" Rhamas asked, his voice full of concern.

"What?" The woman who answered had been pulling a stack of papers onto a board that held things together.

"The mothers?" Rhamas asked again. "Where are they?"

"Oh," she looked around at all the squirming pink and blue bundles.

"Why, they are in their rooms, of course. The babies will be brought to them at feeding time."

Rhamas had never heard the term 'feeding time' used in reference to newborns, but he didn't want to appear stupid, so he just nodded and forced a smile.

"Of course," he said. "Where I come from, the women have the babies in their home and feed the babies whenever they get hungry."

He hoped he was saying it correctly. His English wasn't very good.

"Oh? And, where is that?"

"What?"

"Where are you from, Mr. Whitley?"

The woman who must be a nurse or doctor was smiling, but Rhamas felt threatened. What was he supposed to say to her? Where was he supposed to be from? He didn't know the names of Earth places. Should he say 'Annapolis' or 'Odenton'?

The silence grew awkward, however, and the woman just shook her head and handed him the board with papers on it. The papers had words and numbers on them.

Rhamas had been taught how to read a few words and letters, but these papers had too many. He could feel the heat growing in his face and neck. His eyes watered with humiliation.

"I am not so good with English words." He stammered. "I am sorry that I am not able to write these."

Why did Alisha send me with this woman to do papers? Where is my wife? Will they take my baby if I do not work the marks where they go?

"Can you tell me, where is my wife?"

"Oh. The doctors still needed to fix her up a bit. I'm sure she will be in recovery soon, and I will take you to see her. How would that be?"

"I want to be with her, please. Now."

"Well, Mr. Whitley…"

"I am not this Mr. Whitley you say to me so much! My name is Rhamas of the Jurrah tribe and we do not leave our wives alone when they need us so importantly."

"Ah. How do you spell that?"

"What?"

"Your name, 'Rhamas?'"

"Give me a paper and a pen, please." Rhamas was very proud of the fact that he was able to write his name on paper. That was one of the many things he had learned during his time in Maryland following his flight from the Wise Man of the Agrigar.

"There," Rhamas said, proudly handing the slip of paper back to the nurse. That is the writing of the letters of Rhamas."

"Aha! Thank you, Mr. Rhamas! I'll be sure to call you by the correct name from now on."

Rhamas nodded. The charge nurse then proceeded to type out a label for the baby's bassinet. It read, "Baby Girl, Rhamas."

"Now, I must take my baby back to my wife."

"Well, um, you can't see her just now…"

"I am to go back to room with doctors and wife. I will take baby. You have so many babies. I take this one. Okay?"

Rhamas reached into the bassinet cart and took his daughter fully into his arms for the first time.

A thrill of unbridled joy coursed through him at the feel of her. He smiled at the eyes of her mother and laughed as she stuck out the tip of her very tiny tongue.

"I'm afraid I can't let you do that, Mr. Rhamas. The infants need to stay in the nursery until feeding time."

Rhamas, determined to exert his rights as the baby's father, turned on his heel and walked out without paying the charge nurse any further heed.

"Security! I need your help in Maternity right now!"

Rhamas looked up to see the middle-aged woman speaking tensely into a telephone. When she looked up, her eyes were angry and suspicious, but also prematurely victorious.

He turned on his heel and strode off in the direction of the operating room where he had last seen Alisha. The woman screeched something after him about how he was going to get 'arrested' for kidnapping? Rhamas wondered why holding a sleeping baby was making her so upset, but only picked up speed.

Rhamas needed to find Alisha. He didn't like making babies in a hospital. *This is not a good thing, keeping mother and father and baby in different places. I will find Alisha and take her home where I can keep her safe.*

Arrest Him!

Dawn broke in Natalo II and the morning sun sketched patches of moving sunlight onto Matthew's sleeping form. He lay on his side with his knees tucked up tight. His breathing was deep and even, with an occasional snort or gruffle and tendrils of his hair lifted slightly with the passing of each little breeze.

Standing nearby and staring down at him, three Jurrah huntsmen by the names of Shakmun, Brisballah, and Nemanic grinned malevolently.

"We have caught the human murderer!" exclaimed Nemanic in a whisper.

"Let them say that we are too stupid to find him, now, eh?" Brisballah added. "Shh. He moves."

"The human has no legs! Do you fear he will outrun us?"

Shakmun spoke this last at full volume and with an imperious tone. As the leader of this expedition, he was clearly unconcerned about whether or not the guilty creature should awaken as a result.

"The one we look for had legs enough to run – long and hard he ran. Could this not be a different human?" Brisballah, the most intelligent of the three, pointed out.

"We will take him with us. The Chieftain will decide." Shakmun said with a glare.

"Of course! He is human. Is that not a crime in itself?" Nemanic played up to Shakmun at every opportunity, and this was his chance to put Brisballah in a bad light.

"If he is our human, where has he been? Could he have been hiding in these woods for over a year?"

"No. We would have found him, or he would surely have starved. This human must have been portal jumping and decided to come back for something."

"To this soulless place, without legs? For what would he return? Do you see about him any precious objects? Gold? Jewels?"

"Brisballah, you trouble yourself over nothing. These are not questions we were sent to ask. Our purpose is to collect the criminal and deliver him for trial."

"This is just a boy. Do you not see? He looks too young and innocent to be anybody's murderer."

"What is he to you? Can I ask that? What is this legless human boy to you that he must be defended so?" Nemanic saw that his attack on Brisballah was gaining Shakmun's approval, so he wasted no time in ramping up his verbal assault.

"He is nothing to me," Brisballah refused to be drawn in. "I say only that I feel he is not the same creature we were sent to find."

"So? What if he isn't the same boy? How do we know that he will not kill someone or steal something in the future? It has been proven that humans are all criminals by nature."

"The boy has no legs."

"I can see that. Do you think that I cannot see as well as you?"

"I am just saying that…"

"I hear your words, Brisballah! Do you hear the words I am saying? I am saying that we have found a human where humans don't belong. We must take him with us for questioning. We are honor-bound to do that, do you not agree?"

"Shakmun, noble leader, we take the chance of being judged foolish for arresting this child with no legs," Brisballah argued.

"Foolish! Do you say with your mouth I am foolish?" Nemanic stepped into Brisballah's space and waved his arms about, emphatically.

"Nemanic." Brisballah said calmly with a measured step backward.

"What?"

"The evil, legless boy murderer is awake and he is smiling at us."

Code Blue

Alisha Whitley sat up to find out what all of the excitement was about. The doctors and nurses were getting louder by the minute and everyone was making frantic grabs for bizarre pieces of equipment.

Hey. Hello? I'm okay. See? I'm sitting up! I'm waving my arms at you. Hello?

Alisha wanted to find Rhamas and the baby. She felt confused and lightheaded, but slid off the table and onto her feet without losing her balance.

Okay. Thanks for everything you did. You guys were great. I would love to hang around, but my husband doesn't do well in places like this, and well, I'd like to hold my daughter. You understand, right?

Okay. I'm leaving now. Good luck with whatever you're having bad luck with. Thanks a million! Bye now.

With a growing feeling of unease, Alisha walked through the operating room doors and down the hallway, following signs to the nursery. She was barefooted and wearing very little, which usually would have embarrassed her to death, but Alisha felt a curious lack of anxiety at the moment.

It was wonderful to be well for the first time in almost a year! Alisha smiled broadly and patted her flattened tummy.

Having a baby isn't anywhere near as awful as I thought it would be. Sure, the pregnancy was lousy, but...

Suddenly, Rhamas turned a corner and ran right through her, carrying the baby.

Rhamas? Where are you going? I'm right here! Honestly, Rhamas, you ran right through me! Hey! Come back here!

Alisha rubbed her eyes and pulled her hair away from her face. She wasn't thinking straight. It was probably side effects from the anesthesia.

Wow. He was really moving. I'd better try to catch up with him and find out what's wrong, she thought.

Honestly. I love the man more than life itself, but he does find ways to make things difficult.

Alisha's feet weren't touching the floor anymore, but

that hadn't seemed unusual to her in the least. As a matter of fact, it had made joining Rhamas and the baby much easier.

Hmm, that's nice. This explains why so many people are addicted to narcotics. Feeling all 'floaty' and 'hover-ish-y' would be easy to get used to.

Alisha, Rhamas and their newborn daughter were standing in the operating room. Tears were running down Rhamas's cheeks as he watched the commotion surrounding a deathly pale body on the operating table.

Rhamas? Why are you crying? Rhamas? Look at me, my love. Why is everyone so sad?

Alisha stepped up to the operating table and saw something very strange.

Herself.

Anarchy

"Hello?"

Tori Chandler had been standing at the nurse's station for a full minute, but not one of the three nurses working within sight of her had bothered to look up.

For a brief period, Tori had considered reaching over the desk and tapping one of them on the shoulder, but in the end, she hadn't had the nerve.

"Excuse me," Mrs. Whitley stepped up and elected to give it a try. "Hello?"

The response to her salutation was underwhelming.

The underwhelming-ness went on for an inordinately long time.

"Screw it," Tori said, grabbing Carolyn's arm. "Let's just go straight to his room."

"But, we still don't know what he's in here for, and…"

"I promise, if your husband doesn't have a chart hanging on the end of his bed, or sitting in a folder somewhere nearby, we'll find someone to ask."

"But, shouldn't we tell them we're here?"

"If they don't care why we're here, then why should we care to tell them anything?"

Carolyn seemed to consider this for a minute before changing her expression from one of rigid conformity to the very definition of 'Screw It.'

(A photo of someone facially expressing this sentiment can be found in *The Complete Guide to an Antiestablishment Adulthood, Chapter 6,* under "I tried to do it your way…").

The pair of rebels marched straight to room #112, (okay, they might have made one wrong turn, but it is common knowledge that hospitals thrive on keeping people in a constant state of confusion).

"Here it is." Carolyn whispered.

"Do you want me to wait?"

"Absolutely not," Carolyn replied, giving her unruly hair a smooth and a pat. "Tori, I'm scared out of my mind right now."

"C'mon. Pull up your big-girl panties and let's go."

Mrs. Whitley pushed her way through the door to room #112, peered in and were met with the sight of the myriad of jumbled tubes, leads and monitors surrounding a bed.

Tori, quickly running out of patience, snatched the chart out of a plastic pocket on the wall outside the room before nudging Matthew's mother over the threshold and into the presence of a very sick Grant Whitley.

"Oh my God..."

This is the wrong room. That can't be my husband. This man is a different color, and his lips are as blue as a cadaver's. Carolyn stepped closer to make sure. *That isn't Grant. Is it?*

One glance at the dying man's claw-like hands had resolved the question.

"That woman downstairs must have given us the wrong room. This must be the other Whitley. It's not Grant. We're going to have to go back and find out where they put him."

"Carolyn?"

Shocked, Carolyn whipped her head around to see that the patient's eyes had opened.

"Tori?"

"Grant?"

The instant that the awareness of the patient's true identity completed its leap from one synapse to another, Carolyn's face lost all color, her eyes rolled back in her head, and Grant Whitley's emotionally-taxed wife collapsed.

Take me to your Leader

Matthew dreamed he was at home and had left the television on. As the volume increased, however, his dreaming-self had sat up to grab the remote before one of his parents could march down the hall in a lecture frame of mind.

By the time he had focused enough to realize that he wasn't alone, Matthew was actually relieved to see the three men that were gathered nearby, clearly, arguing over what should be done with him.

These guys must be the Jurrahs that Alisha wrote about in her journal. I'll bet they can take me to the Agrigar village on Natalo I. It would be great to see an Agrigar. Wow.

They are a friendly tribe. Nothing to worry about.

Besides, they will like me a lot better once they know I'm Alisha's brother. She married one of them, after all. What was his name? Remus? No. Started with an 'R.'

Matthew dug into his back pocket for his wallet and

pulled out the photo of Alisha he had kept there since she had disappeared just over two years ago.

The three Jurrahs – if they were, in fact, Jurrahs as Matthew suspected – were arguing so strenuously that they seemed completely unaware of the fact that he was wide awake and sitting up. He took some time to look them over.

One of them, the really hairy-faced guy, was standing back to observe the other two as they bickered. He was wiry and stood by with his arms crossed in front of his chest and his feet planted a foot apart.

That guy must be their boss. Matthew thought.

He stood like a boss – kind of' full of himself.

Of the other two, one was loud and obnoxious and the other – the chubbier one – was coming off as the know-it-all, reasonable type.

Like me.

Matthew was grinning at his own powers of astute observation when the nerdy Jurrah met his eyes. He waved and smiled at the three of them with what he hoped was his most engaging expression.

I come in peace. Take me to your leader. Matthew

thought, trying to interject his friendly intentions into every facial muscle.

Uh oh. There isn't any smiling and waving going on over there. What do I do, now?

Matthew's smile froze and his face flushed hot.

The picture, idiot! Show them the picture! "It's okay, guys. I'm Alisha's brother. Look."

He offered the photo to the more intelligent of the three, who did come forward to take it – ever so gingerly – from Matthew's fingers.

"Alisha? Remus (at least I think it's Remus)? Do you know who I'm talking about? Friends? Alisha and Remus are friends."

Matthew gulped, nervously and his eyes began to water. This genius plan wasn't having the desired effect.

Instead, the chubby one had gasped when he saw what was on the paper, and showed the others with a mix of horror and admiration.

They've never seen a photograph before, you moron. You'll be lucky if they don't burn you at the stake for a witch. Crap.

Matthew Whitley watched helplessly as the three male whatevers quarreled wildly, throwing him occasional glares of suspicion and hatred.

I should run. He thought, suddenly frantic. *What am I saying? I can't run. I can't walk. Hard to see how my cracker-jack scuttling skills are going to help...*

When the man-things approached him cautiously with a length of rope, Matthew could only sigh and allow himself to be trussed up and suspended from a sturdy branch like a pig on his way to the roasting pit.

Okay. Okay. This sucks. Maximum suckage. Smart boy just had to have an adventure.

Shit-crackers.

I See You

Grant Whitley had no worries. The morphine drip was keeping him happy, and he was tucked neatly into bed all comfy and cozy in a private room with hardwood floors and an amazing view of the parking lot.

This is what we called "Better living through chemistry" in the 60's, he chuckled. *Oh. Nope, nope. It was "Trendy chemical amusement!"*

Still, every now and then, Grant would have a troubling feeling that he was forgetting something. Those moments were short-lived, which was nice, but he knew there had to be something – something really serious – that he should be attending to right now.

Probably why I had a 'myocardial' whatsit in the first place, and best forgotten. He tried to convince himself.

I need to step back from the everyday stresses of life and take care of my own health. My body needs me. Yep.

My turn, my turn, my turn Miss-Carolyn--of-the-

constantly-in-crisis. Ha-ha-ha-ha.

That's so funny. I'm a funny guy.

"How are you doing, Mr. Whitley?"

A pretty Asian tech wheeled into the room with an electrical tower of some sort and pulled a blood pressure cuff off the side.

"Me? Oh, I'm feeling no pain."

"So, on a scale of 1-10, would you say your pain is a zero?"

"Zero. Yep. That's what I said."

The cuff went from tight to *oh-my-god-what-are-you-trying-to-do-take-off-my-arm?*

"Hmm. Your blood pressure is high."

"It gets that way when I'm suffering an unexpected amputation of the arm," he said.

The twenty-something slip of a girl had a nametag that said "Sandy."

"Sandy, I think your cuff might need replacing. That's not supposed to cause bone fractures and induce screams of agony."

Sandy laughed, without humor, and said, "We'll try

again later."

"Can't wait," Grant quipped, his voice dripping with sarcasm.

The lithe and lovely Sandy clamped something onto his middle finger (next time he'd hold it up just to be extra helpful) and stuck a digital thermometer into his mouth, simultaneously.

Those readings must have been up to snuff, because Sandy flashed him a perky smile and threatened joyfully to 'come back in an hour' before wheeling her cart of curiosities off to torture some other poor sod in a hospital gown.

Grant was still shaking his head when another member of the hospital staff darkened his door.

"Hello, Mr. Whitley. We're going to need to take some blood from you today."

"Oh, joy," he replied, dead pan.

"Could you spell your last name for me?"

"It spells the way it sounds."

"I still need for you to spell it. Sorry. Hospital procedures."

"Okay. G-R-A-N-T W-H-I-T-L-E-Y," Grant spelled out loud in all caps, mildly irritated.

"Is that two 'Ts" or one?"

"Did I say two "Ts?"

"So, one "T" then."

"You're good."

"Thank you, and your birthdate?"

"October 18...."

"And the year?"

"I think I'm going to vomit."

"What?"

"Get me something to vomit into! It must be the morphine. I'm going to…"

Grant heaved ceaselessly into his lap for several minutes and when he finally raised his eyes, the nurse was still standing by her keyboard like a statue -- unmoving -- as though she hadn't moved a muscle. Her round face wore an expression of disgust.

"Might I have some tissues or paper towels to wipe up my face? Perhaps a cup of water?"

"I'll get the tech," Nurse Sandy said between tight

lips.

The woman's abrupt exit afforded Grant a view of her wide, flat, uniform-draped buttocks as they marched obstinately out of sight.

Grant sat in his private room and waited for the promised tech to arrive. Minutes passed. He had already wiped his mouth on the hem of his gown, given no other options. The weight of his vomit pressed into his lap and the resulting moisture slowly began to seep through the sheets and onto his legs.

Is anybody coming to help me with this mess? Are they making me sit in it as a kind of punishment for daring to vomit in the first place?

Grant looked around for a call button and couldn't find one. He was connected to a monitor via an octopus of wire leads, and an IV was power-strapped to his right wrist.

Well, they've got me roped in. I'm not going anywhere.

Finally, coming to the correct conclusion that no help was forthcoming, Grant rolled his soiled bedding up into a kind-of vomit burrito and 'heaved' it overboard.

Ha! 'Heaved it.' I don't care what anybody says, I

am a funny man. There. At least I'm not sitting in it.

That still left Grant with the issue of a vomit-smeared gown, a mouth that tasted like a mash-up of yesterday's lunch plus the hind-end of a camel, and a bed with no coverings in a chilly room.

"Where is that call button? It must be around here, somewhere."

Then, he saw it. There, a nurse's cap with a red plus sign was stamped over a button among the bed controls on a side rail.

Gotcha! Mr. Whitley pressed the button and was gratified to hear a static-enriched voice in reply.

"Can I help you?" it asked.

"Yes, please. I have made a mess on my sheets and I need help getting cleaned up."

Grant felt mildly humiliated hearing his voice over the loudspeaker as he begged for help with messy sheets.

"Oh? How did that happen?"

Truly? She wants me to confess my 'transgression' to the entire floor?

"Could you please send a tech to my room?"

"Yes. She's not on the ward at the moment, but I'll send her as soon as she gets back."

"Thanks."

Right. I'm on my own over here. Got it. He thought.

One at a time, Grant Whitley removed the leads that were adhered to his body.

He supposed that there was a monitor somewhere that told the nurse's station he had just died. For some reason, the lack of interest that ensued did not come as a surprise.

The IV pole could be rolled along with him, so he opted to leave the line in his hand alone for the time being.

Once out of bed and on his feet, Grant began to rifle through the various drawers hidden behind the closet doors.

"Aha! There you are," he exclaimed aloud upon locating the hospital gowns.

The next drawer down held blankets and sheets. There was a harvest-gold plastic bin on the seat of an easy chair, filled with assorted grooming items. Grant lifted out a plastic-encased tooth brush and a sample-sized tube of toothpaste.

We're doing this, he congratulated himself, dropping the fresh sheet and blanket onto his bed before attempting to tow the IV pole, fresh gown, comb, toothbrush and toothpaste into the attached bathroom.

Grant didn't make it. There was a problem. The electrical cord belonging to his IV pole was not long enough to get where he was going, so he was going to have to unplug the bastard.

Oh crap, he was getting tired. *Nothing in this place is going to be easy.*

But, Mr. Whitley didn't get through law school and pass the Bar exams without growing a substantial backbone.

He located the outlet -- hidden behind his headboard and nearly a foot above the floor -- where it would require a superhuman effort to dislodge. Grant sucked in a deep breath and tapped into his inner Batman. In no time, the plug was draped safely over the IV monitor and he was free to move about the 'cabin.'

Grant Whitley wheeled the cumbersome IV pole into the bathroom with the idea of ridding himself of all traces of yuck.

He was a bit unsteady on his feet, but was also glowing with a sense of pride at his gargantuan achievements.

Keep your damned tech. See? I can clean up after my own self.

The image that greeted him in the bathroom mirror was shocking. Grant Whitley, Esq. regarded a reinforced bandage across a swollen nose, the beginnings of two spectacular shiners, and a smattering of ugly abrasions across his chin and cheeks – (one of which still boasted an imbedded crumb of parking lot).

Grant sighed, gingerly brushed his teeth and splashed water on his face. He dampened and combed his wild hair into some semblance of order, then filled his joined hands four times with cold tap water and drank deeply.

Next, Grant attempted to remove his dirty hospital gown.

Great. Just great. I'm about to lose my temper, and nobody wants for that to happen.

Grant clenched his teeth and attempted to breathe deeply through them. It made a satisfying hissing sound.

The gown could not be removed over the IV tubing. Grant was going to have to disconnect the blasted thing after all.

Still breathing deeply, Grant sat on the toilet and examined the tubing. There was a juncture a few inches from the insertion point that appeared to unscrew. Grant twisted the two ends until he was free of the pole and ignored the pool of liquid that was gathering under the loose end.

He wasn't bothered by the puddle. It felt too good to be free.

Gratefully, Grant began to slip off his soiled robe before unfolding the new one.

SHIT! Grant cursed internally.

The freshly-laundered version was not much more than an oddly-shaped mat of blue-flecked fabric bordered by a puzzle of assorted snaps and ties. What was he supposed to do with that?

It was nearly impossible to secure all of it with no assistance, and Grant was just so tired. He needed to go back to bed. He couldn't fight this mess for one more second.

But, he had to face the fact that he was alone. Nobody was coming to help him, and he wasn't about to walk around naked, so Grant worked patiently to sort and snap this bit to that bit until he felt he was appropriately attired and completely exhausted.

The entire process now needed to be reversed in order to restore 'peace to the land.'

Grant scooped up extra gowns, sheets and blankets to store in the drawer of his bedside table – just in case.

The hardest part of the return-to-bed process was getting the IV plug back into the outlet behind his bed. It took four tries, but Grant managed to do it on the fifth, and as soon as he lay back down, he was asleep.

The still-folded bedding was cuddled to his chest when the tech came back for his blood pressure, temperature and respirations.

"Mr. Whitley? Sorry to wake you, but I need your vital signs. Mr. Whitley?"

Grant fought his way up from a black well of sleep and focused on the girl bleary-eyed.

"Yes?"

"Hello, Mr. Whitley. How are you feeling? Do you

have any pain? Could you give your pain a number from 1 to 10, with 10 being the most pain you have ever experienced? Let's get your blood pressure," Sandy said, cheerily, pulling the evil cuff from the side of her cart.

It's Alive

Tori jumped. The thing that was hooked up to all of the wires and tubes had spoken.

"Carolyn? Tori?"

Tori turned to look back at it and saw the open eyes and enquiring face of no other than Matthew's father, Grant Whitley, Esquire.

Wow. He didn't look like himself.

"Hi, Mr. Whitley. We got here as soon as we could."

"What happened?" Carolyn rushed to his bedside and took his hand in hers.

"He had a myocardial infarction in the parking lot." Tori read from Mr. Whitley's chart.

"Oh, Grant!" Carolyn exclaimed. "I feel so awful about not being there when you needed me."

"Not there? What do you mean? Where were you? I

honestly don't remember anything about how I got here," he offered, freeing his hand from hers to smooth some rebel hairs out of his face. "The last thing I recollect is sitting in my office and…"

"Someone left a message on my phone that you had been brought into the hospital by a young man." Carolyn said.

"A young man?"

Carolyn's comment made Grant's heart race. It was distressing, but he couldn't figure out why.

There was a memory dancing just outside his diminished circle of light...

"Young man? I can't imagine."

Tori watched Mr. Whitley's pulse rate rise on the monitor above his bed and indicated her concern to Mrs. Whitley with a nod in its direction.

"That doesn't matter, now, does it? Maybe it was a guy that found you in the parking lot and helped you inside."

"Yes. That must be it." Carolyn agreed. "Really, honey, it's nothing to worry yourself over."

"How are you feeling? Do you have any idea how long they are going to keep you?"

Mr. Whitley closed his eyes and appeared to be sleeping.

"No. I haven't seen a doctor since they brought me up here. They are giving me morphine, so I sleep a lot."

"Are you in pain?" Carolyn's brow furrowed.

"Not now. That's what the morphine is for." Grant laughed, weakly.

"I was in the yard – um – enjoying the beautiful day when you called. When I checked my phone, I found that you had called several times asking me to call back, and you sounded so upset, that I was going to dial you back, immediately, but then I got that message from the hospital saying that a young man had brought in a family member."

Carolyn was wound up and talking non-stop. Tori could see Mr. Whitley's heart rate meter rising in correspondence with the speed of her prattling.

"Can I get you anything, Mr. Whitley? Are you thirsty?"

"Oh, Tori, you are an angel! I have been asking for ice water since I got here, and everybody says they'll be right back, or they'll ask my nurse, or… Oh, never mind all that. Yes, I would love some water. Tap would be fine if you can't find anything else.

"They have a fridge in the hall with cups of ice water and straws." Tori said. "I can't imagine why nobody brought one to you, unless…" Tori hesitated. "I'd better make sure you're allowed to have it. Sometimes they have frozen lollipops for patients who have restrictions. I'll find out for you and be right back."

"Good luck getting anybody to notice you're alive," he warned, "or dead, for that matter."

Tori made her way down the hall until she reached the First floor nursing station. She had been fully prepared to jump into somebody's lap and sing the Star Spangled Banner if she encountered more of their unapologetic apathy, but she was in luck. Two nurses were talking over a chart and actually looked up as Tori approached.

"Can we help you?" the blonde one asked, smiling.

"Yes. Thank you. I am visiting my, um, father in 112. He asked me to get him some ice water, but I don't know if he is allowed to have it."

"112? That's the one that came in today, right?" The

blonde nurse smiled, prettily.

"That's right." Tori nodded.

"Who is his nurse?" The second nurse, a thirty-something brunette with huge eyes joined the conversation.

"Um. I don't know. I haven't been here very long, so…" Tori gulped, hoping she hadn't run smack dab into a "whining-type" situation, after all. "But, he is very thirsty…"

"I'll and bring him some water, if he isn't NPO." The perky blonde volunteered.

"Um. Okay."

What the hell is 'NPO?' Tori thought.

"If he can't have water, could you please bring him some of those lollipop things? He is very thirsty."

Was that whining? Am I now whining for water? Is that what's happening here?

"Sure. No worries. I'll get his nurse."

So, we're back to "I'll get his nurse" again, are we? Great. Why do I get the feeling that this man is going to die thirsty?

"Will it take long? I told him I'd bring him some water right away, and…" Tori knew she was whining, and she hated people who whined, but she had promised that she would cut through the bull and get him some fricking ice water, and she was pretty sure these girls were feeding her a line of bull.

"I mean, I'd be happy to take it to him, if you guys are busy..."

The nurses exchanged looks. "Okay. Let me make sure he can have it." The one with the brunette braid hanging halfway down her back walked over to a monitor and clicked some keys.

"He is okay for liquids today" she said over her shoulder.

"Great! I'll just take one from the fridge over there?"

"Sure, honey. That's fine. Thanks, we have been understaffed today, and it can be pretty crazy on this floor."

Before they could get back to comparing notes over their prom dresses, or whatever, Tori was already down the hall and pulling a large Styrofoam cup out of the fridge, so the last bit fell clear of her radar.

Right, busy, but we're talking about a cup of water that was already sitting here. Really? Like nobody could get him a drink of water?

"Where's Matthew?"

Tori overheard the question as she walked in.

"Here's your water! I checked, and you are okay to have it, so drink up! I can get you some more when you finish that one."

"Oh! That's so great, you have no idea how dry I am!"

Grant accepted the drink and sucked it down in huge gulps.

"So, when do you get fed around here?" Carolyn asked, trying to steer the conversation away from their son.

"I know nothing. They come in here to take blood and get my vital statistics and then they disappear. My call button hasn't been much help."

"Is it broken?"

"Only on the human end," he said, sarcastically.

"The nurses told me that they were understaffed."

"Apparently," Grant's eyes began to close again.

"Why don't you rest while I take Tori home, and then I'll come back and stay with you for a while."

It wasn't a question.

"Sounds fine. I'm pretty tired. Can you bring me a couple more cups of water, just in case there is a shortage after you leave?"

"I'm on it," Tori went to fetch them. "Okay. I'll leave now so I can get back faster," Carolyn kissed her husband on the forehead and turned to leave.

"Here you are!" Tori set a supply of iced water on the tray table and wished him a quick recovery, but Grant Whitley had already fallen asleep.

No more than two minutes later a very tall black male tech wheeled into Mr. Whitley's room with a cart of gadgets.

"Mr. Whitley? How are you feeling? Do you have any pain? Could you give your pain a number between 1 and 10, with 10 being the most pain you've ever felt? I need you to sit up so I can get your vitals."

Grant could see the same threadbare blood pressure cuff hanging threateningly from its perch on the cart.

He sighed.

Hit me (Baby) One More Time

The surgeon told everyone in the room to get back.

"Clear!" he said. Then, he hit Alisha with another charge of electricity in the hopes of restarting her heart.

I need to get back into my body! Alisha thought, frantically. *Like, a while ago!*

As quickly as 'inhumanly' possible (which is pretty fast, actually) Alisha rejoined her body.

"Okay. One more time, then we're calling it," the surgeon spoke gently, but looked away from Rhamas as he spoke.

"Clear!"

Once again the paddles were placed on either side of Alisha's heart and the current lifted her unresponsive body into a controlled spasm that was hard to watch.

Every eye was glued to the monitor for a heartbeat, but the line that represented Alisha's life force remained flat and unchanged.

Then, something happened. There was a blip on the screen. It was followed by another. Then, one more blip skipped across the thin white line that held her future in its geometry.

"We've got a pulse!" somebody yelled out.

"She is alive? Is she? Is my wife yet living?" Rhamas implored any one of the blue-paper-people to answer.

"Why is he in here?" the surgeon asked, tersely. One of the nurses walked over to where Rhamas was standing.

"She is alive, for now," she said, taking him by the arm and leading him out of the operating room.

"Your wife lost a lot of blood during the birth, and she almost died, but we are giving her new blood and the surgeons are working hard to stop any more from leaking out so that she will get stronger and stay alive."

"But, I just saw her as a dead woman with eyes of stone." Rhamas said, running the back of one hand across his eyes to wipe away tears.

"Yes, you did, but the doctors were able to start her heart up again, and now she must go to a special place in the hospital where there are machines to help her breathe and tubes to feed her until she feels better.

"I must stay with her," Rhamas said, knowing that the hospital probably wouldn't allow it.

"Let the doctors do their job, okay?"

"Okay," he said, straining to look behind him at Alisha's pale form.

"Aren't you two supposed to be in the nursery?"

"The woman there called the men to come and catch me. She does not want me to have my own baby? Is this not a crazy thing?"

"Ah. Don't worry. I'll come with you and explain everything."

"You are fine woman, worthy of my tribe, and I am large of heart for your kind good to me. I think you would make fine wife for my father. Do you go through the stone?"

The operating room nurse, Lucille Bertrand, smiled warmly, having no idea what this man was talking about, and shook her head thinking that it must be very hard for this man of simple ways to navigate their institutionalized setting.

With patience, she guided Rhamas back to the nursery where one angry charge nurse and two frustrated security guards were pacing the floor.

"That's him! That's Mr. Whitley! Arrest him!"

"That won't be necessary, Margaret," Lucille said. "Dr. Nuissari has excused this man's actions, under the circumstances. We nearly lost his wife just now, and Rhamas is not from our country and is very confused by our customs."

"That's okay, boys. Thank you. I guess it was a false alarm. Everything seems to have been resolved satisfactorily," the charge nurse mumbled under her breath.

"Hello. We are here again," said Rhamas, flashing his killer smile with a tear-stained face. "I will try to understand the paper marks, now. They give me a very bad headache."

The charge nurse suddenly found this handsome young man irresistibly adorable, and in spite of her best intentions, all of her righteous indignation seeped out of her starched button holes and into the weave of the carpeting.

"Which of these should my baby go into?" Rhamas asked, bewildered by the number of bassinets that were now available.

"You can hold her, if you want to. You are her daddy, after all. Let's get busy on this paperwork, okay? I'll be happy to read it for you and write down your answers.

"I will try very hard. Yes. Thank you," Rhamas smiled brightly as he cradled his new daughter in his arms.

'Trussed' in Me

The crude ropes cut into the tender backs of Matthew's knees as he swung helplessly from side to side. His wrists were raw and bleeding. Even if he could have freed his stumps from the lines, his hands would still have been bound tightly and he would probably be made to drag along on the treacherous forest floor.

I shouldn't have shown them the photo. Matthew thought, with regret. *I think I was winning them over until they got hold of that. Dumb, dumb, dumb.*

His three captors spoke little, and what little they did have to say was mostly made up of grunts, clicks and garbled nonsense. The one in charge marched in front with his head held high and his hands free, while the two underlings struggled and grunted under Matthew's weight.

Should I tell them about my chair? I don't want to leave it here. Will they be impressed by the technology of it, or just more convinced than ever that I'd make a tasty shish-ka-bob?

Matthew noticed for the first time that they weren't taking the same path. As a matter of fact, they seemed to be heading in the completely opposite direction.

Where are they taking me? There isn't a settlement on Natalo II, only the fields, the forest, and the Ghama Traya, right?

The tallest trees Matthew had ever seen towered above them so high that they seemed to pierce the clouds, and the morning sun's rays burst through the canopy and between the massive trunks intermittently as though God Himself was using spotlights to search him out.

It would have been a spectacular sight, but for the current circumstances Matthew found himself in.

I'll need my chair, he thought, frantically. *But if I leave it, perhaps Tori or Alisha will come upon it and know I was here... What am I thinking! I can't let them take me without my chair!*

"Wait!" Matthew screamed at the top of his voice. "STOP!" Matthew's captors stopped dead in their tracks and fixed him with questioning glares.

"Back! Go that way! It is important! That way, please! I need my chair!"

Having no other way to point his desired path, Matthew jerked his head towards the forest's entrance.

Brisballah's bright blue eyes caught Matthew's meaning, instantly.

"The boy wants us to move that way. He needs to show us something."

"Unfortunately for him, Jurrah Huntsmen do not accept commands from lowly human prisoners," Nemanic declared, haughtily.

With an insolent 'Huff', Nemanic shouldered his half of the burden and made as if to continue on their chosen path.

"Stop! You must take me back to my chair! I can't move without it! Go that way!"

Matthew's whole body thrashed in protest of Nemanic's refusal to comply, causing the Jurrahs to let go of the pole from which he was suspended and drop him unceremoniously onto a small thorn bush with very large thorns.

"Ouch! Get me off of this thing! What's the matter

with you people! I'm being stabbed in about a hundred places! Get me off of this damned bush!"

"What is the matter with this human? Didn't I tell you that he is dangerous, and must be imprisoned or put to death as soon as possible?"

"Be quiet, all of you!" Shakmun commanded from his forward position. "Are you children? You bicker and carry on in a most distressing way. I will have no more of it."

The three transgressors, Matthew included, fell silent and dropped their eyes.

"Brisballah, what is all of this commotion about? Why have we stopped, and why is this child on the ground?"

"The boy is most insistent that he be taken the other way. He seems to have left a most valuable possession, and refuses to be borne further without first acquiring it."

"Of course, we will not bow to this little snelbista!" Nemanic jumped in to add. "If he will not remain still, we will simply have to knock him over the head until he is senseless."

Shakmun ran a hand along his hairy cheeks and

downward the length of his substantial beard. He seemed to be considering their options.

Matthew, still in pain and needing rescue, did his best to let his captors in on his pointy dilemma.

"Hello? I am sitting on a bed of ICE PICKS over here!"

"Nemanic. Come and assist me. The boy is sitting in a Juthraki bush."

"Let him bleed. I care not about the suffering of hoodlums."

"Assist the boy," Shakmun ordered in a quiet voice that carried with it a certain menace. "Untie him and see to his injuries. Do it, now."

"But, Master…"

"The boy has courage. Besides the more I think about it, Brisballah speaks wise words. We will appear as fools if we put this child before the court. It is clear that he is not the man we seek."

"But the girl! He has the paper of the Alisha, and speaks of her husband, Rhamas! He is a conspirator! We must deal with him before he…"

Shakmun raised a large, hairy hand and slapped the weasel-like-rat-nosed face of Nemanic before another word whine past his considerable overbite.

"I will have silence! This matter has been considered carefully, and a decision has been made. I will not take this human to our city as a prisoner."

"You are just going to let him go free, Master?"

"No. I am going to take the human to the Agrigar village. I believe that the Wise Man of the Agrigars will pay us a generous sum for him."

"Ah. That is true enough! We shall be made wealthy men by doing as you say! I am sorry for doubting your wisdom, Master."

"As you should be," Shakmun folded his arms over his chest. "It is well known that the wizard wants to get his hands on the Alisha girl and her Jurrah husband. This boy has obviously got some connection to them both."

"Then, we shall travel through the Ghama Traya?" Brisballah asked, shuddering.

There was a long pause as this prospect was considered by all present.

"We have done this before, and we shall do it

again." Shakmun stated with gravity.

"But, never without the Wise Man..." Nemanic blurted.

"That magician's words and brightly-colored sparks are naught but showmanship and twaddle. All that is needed is the correct placement of the hands. We have no need to fear the stone."

Matthew sensed a distinct change of atmosphere amongst his captors. The chubbier, smarter one lifted him off of the thorn bush and gingerly removed the merciless spikes from his nethers.

"Ouch! Oh, that's better," Matthew sighed as each flaming agony subsided. "Thanks."

"Brisballah," whispered the Jurrah, pointing to himself.

"Brisballah? I am Matthew," Our intrepid explorer reciprocated.

"Am I now free?" Matthew made every motion he could think of to represent freedom, but the Jurrah named Brisballah shook his head in what must be a universal "No" and shrugged.

Misty Water-Colored Memories

Grant Whitley, Esquire was asleep in room 112. Anyone watching him would have wondered what kind of dreams would cause such tossing, turning, flinching and loud gibberish-like exclamations. Something terrible was fighting its way to the forefront of his mind. Something he had forgotten. Something... important...

Grant did not see the new patient that was being wheeled into the next room. He was unaware of the life and death struggle that the unidentified patient was battling. He certainly had no idea that he was now a grandfather. Those actualities were swimming against a current of morphine and mayhem and not likely to surface any time soon.

Instead, Mr. Whitley wrestled away rogue blood-pressure cuffs the size of Great Danes and dodged villainous, blood-sucking syringes, jabbing wherever he did not have a vein and performing 360 degree sweeps under his skin – just because.

Grant's IV monitor had started beeping obnoxiously some while ago, but, if he heard it at all, the blaaat, blaaat, blaaat was nothing but another thread in the fabric of his nightmares.

The voices blended together and called from every side.

"What is your pain level, Mr. Whitley? Can you give it a number from 1 to 10?" the blood cuff asked, solicitously as it threatened to squeeze the life out of him.

"I'm going to need a little blood today, Mr. Whitley," the vampiress in white hissed through curved fangs. Through his spinning, morphine-fueled brain a series of disturbing words echoed eerily: *"There is a young man here who has just brought your daughter into the emergency room."*

A young man? A young man has my daughter. Why does a young man have my daughter? My daughter? My daughter is not here. She is in another place. Another place.

Grant struggled to snap back into the present moment and willed his eyes to narrow the nurse into better focus.

"How is your pain, Mr. Whitley?" The parrot-in-white seemed to squawk out the words.

"I'm going to need to get a little blood from you today."

"Give it a number from 1 to 10."

"Could you please spell your name for me?"

"The woman in the emergency room said there were two Whitley's today."

"What is your date of birth?"

"Two Whitleys. Two Whitleys. Two Whitleys."

Grant thrashed wildly from side to side. His feet became tangled in the linens. Sweat poured from him in droplets that soaked his hair and saturated his poor excuse for a pillow.

"Caesarean Section," a nasal voice emanated from a Fisher Price telephone with moving blue eyes. *"An emergency Caesarean Section."*

No! My daughter isn't having a baby! My daughter is too young to have a baby! She is far away in another place. Alisha can't be in your emergency room. You must have the wrong number! Grant's tortured mind called out to chase the memory away.

"Two Whitleys."

"Your pressure is high. Is it always this high? Do you take any medications for blood pressure? I'll be back in twenty minutes to check it again."

"A young man…"

"Isn't that a coincidence? Two Whitleys in this emergency room on the same day?"

"Can you spell your name for me?"

"I'm going to need a little blood from you today."

"BLAAAT! BLAAAT! BLAAAT!" the apparatus on his IV pole erupted into a series of ear-splitting protestations.

"Whitley? Is that spelled with two 'Ts'?"

A Rose by Any Other Name

Rhamas pulled the tie loose from his shoulder-length, wavy hair and shook his head to free the curls around his face. The nurse lady had been asking him questions and writing down answers for a very long time, and his head was pounding.

"Have you decided on a name, yet?"

"I am sorry, please. What did you say to me?"

"I was just asking if you and your wife had chosen a name for the baby, yet?"

Rhamas' head dropped as he thought about Alisha. The nurse called 'Lu-seel' had promised that she would come and get him once Alisha was settled into a hospital room, but many times passed by him and still he didn't know where to find his only love.

"No," a teardrop fell upon his daughter's tiny face and Rhamas wiped it away with a fingertip. "This we have not done."

She wants me to give our child a Jurrah name. I know that we have spoken of this. Yet, within my people, the name is given by the mother of the wife. I do not know why Alisha's mother does not come to name the baby. Where are the father and the mother and the brother ('Skink,' he thought)?

"Have her mother and father come here?"

"Alisha's parents? No. Have you called them?"

"My wife thought they would be here."

Rhamas dug into his pocket for the wadded-up peanut-butter label and handed it to the nurse called Margaret who accepted it with an indulgent grin.

He is just like a child, she thought. *A big, strong, incredibly-handsome child.*

"Ah. Here are the phone numbers. You and little baby Whitley just wait here. I'll go right now and find out what's keeping them."

Nurse Margaret walked into her office and picked up the receiver. She held the crinkled wrapper up close to her face, but ended up rooting around in her desk drawer for her reading glasses as she couldn't make any sense of what was scribbled there.

"That's better," she muttered, finally making out the smudged digits and punching them into the phone. Margaret cleared her throat as the call connected and the distant ringing tones began. The phone rang through to voicemail, however, and the nurse wasn't sure what she should say. Margaret paused for a moment, before hanging up her extension.

I'll try later, she thought. *They could already be here, you know? They've probably turned their phones off or silenced them.*

"Nobody answered," Nurse Margaret said to Rhamas. "Have you looked for them in the waiting room?"

Rhamas raised his eyes to her, and Margaret could see nothing but question marks in them.

"Do you know where the waiting room is?"

"This I am not sure so much. Also, I do not know their faces. I have never seen them before."

"Ah," Nurse Margaret said, thinking about this. "I know! I will page them to the nursery! If they are in the hospital they will come straight here."

Throne of Chairs

"It is right this way," Matthew explained as he sat comfortably in the linked arms of two of his captors. With hand gestures and encouraging words, he was leading the Jurrahs back towards the forest entrance where he hoped to recover the wheelchair he had left behind.

Matthew knew he might never find out why the three Jurrah huntsmen who had treated him so badly earlier, were now following behind him like obedient ducklings.

Even so, he was pretty sure it had something to do with his new ally, Brisballah.

Whatever the kindly Jurrah had said or done to change the tides, Matthew knew he would be forever in his debt.

After nearly an hour of hiking through the woods, Matthew was finally able to pick out the silhouette of his chair off in the distance.

"There it is!" he exclaimed, excitedly. "There! I see it! Go that way!"

"Thrilling. The boy has found his treasure. Please tell me again of the riches we will be paid for our trouble."

"The portal is not far," said Shakmun. "We will feast among the Agrigars with pockets full of gold."

"Just so we are rid of this loathsome burden," murmured Nemanic just out of hearing.

"What if the Wise Man doesn't wish to purchase the boy?" Brisballah asked. "Will you set him free?"

"I think you like this human too well. Why would we turn such a devil loose upon the peaceful occupants of Natalo I?"

Nemanic had narrowed his eyes and was regarding Brisballah with no small amount of suspicion.

"I have asked for silence where this matter is concerned, and I will not ask again."

Both underlings nodded their assent with pressed lips.

"I see something through the trees." Brisballah said.

"It glints like metal, but I can't make out the shape."

"Is it gold?" Nemanic strained to follow Brisballah's gaze.

"No."

"Is it encrusted with precious gems?"

"I don't think so, but it is too far away to say for certain."

"The human is very excited about this thing, whatever it may be." Shakmun, who couldn't figure out what everyone was looking at, (but wasn't about to admit it), chimed in.

Matthew listened to the indecipherable gobbledygook that passed for his captors' language and wondered what they were saying.

I sure hope this doesn't turn out to be a mistake like the photograph. He thought, grimly. *Regardless of what these guys make of it, I'd be pretty helpless without my chair.*

Perhaps I can switch it on when they aren't looking and make a break for the Ghama Traya?

But Matthew knew he'd be foolish to believe that any wheelchair could make good time over all of that rough terrain.

I'd be lucky not to flip the whole contraption caddy-wompus and break my own neck.

A series of ecstatic explosions – as though a string of cherry bombs had been ignited – jump-started his weary heart and launched Matthew from the arms of his captors to the rough forest floor at their feet.

"My chair!" Matthew exclaimed, knuckling his way to the source of his enthusiasm.

"Grab him!" Nemanic yelled.

"Well, this is a bit of a surprise." Brisballah stood back and observed as the human boy pulled himself up into his elaborate metal throne.

"Back away from the child, you miserable cratznet! Can you not see that he is a King?"

Momma Needs a Milkshake

Carolyn Whitley dozed in and out as she reclined in the chair by Grant's bed. Her husband's fitful thrashings and moanings had made it difficult to get any rest at all, much less anything resembling sleep.

Carolyn had tried multiple times to wake him, but the morphine seemed to have full command of all of Grant's thinking bits.

What on earth is he mumbling about? Whatever has him so upset is nothing compared to the drama he missed out on.

Carolyn had already decided to keep Matthew's whereabouts to herself until she was quite certain that Grant was well enough to take the shock. One dimension-diving child per family was more than any parent could be expected to endure in one lifetime.

Carolyn had managed to flag down a nurse a few hours ago who had assured her that a doctor would be making his rounds later that evening, and that he would be happy to give Carolyn an update on her husband's condition and prognosis.

The large wall clock read 7:00 p.m.

Do doctors even make rounds this late? Carolyn was doubtful.

Suddenly, Grant rolled onto his back and shouted.

"My daughter can't be having a Caesarean section! Isn't that operation for pregnant women? My daughter can't be pregnant! Besides, she is... um... out of town."

Wow. That sounds like some nightmare, Carolyn smirked. *It's that kind of worrying that probably caused him to have a heart attack in the first place.*

Carolyn thanked God that she hadn't been able to answer the phone when she was having her own breakdown! The knowledge of what Matthew had just done would have been all that was needed to put Grant straight into his grave.

"I've got to get to the emergency room! Alisha! I'm coming, honey! Hang on. Daddy's coming!"

Carolyn stood, determined to wake her husband from his troubled sleep, but Grant seemed to settle down as soon as her hand touched his shoulder, and she decided it would be best to let him sleep.

I've got to get out of here, Carolyn thought, running the fingers of one hand through her tousled hair. *I need a shake.*

She really did. It hadn't been a good day, what with seeing her only son pop off the planet and into another reality only to be told immediately after that her husband had just collapsed in the hospital parking lot.

Some people headed to a bar, Carolyn looked for the nearest vanilla shake – the bigger, the better.

Being fully aware that such an item would not be easily procured within the hospital walls, Carolyn turned her cravings elsewhere. She remembered that the hamburger place just down the road now served (pretty darn magnificent) milkshakes, and – with one guilty look at her sleeping hubby – Carolyn Whitley shouldered her purse and took off.

The sooner I go, the sooner I'll get back. She told herself.

Then, before Carolyn had even made it to the hallway, the reality hit her between the eyes.

Oh Lord! Tori drove me to the hospital. I don't have a car!

Still determined to have that milkshake, Carolyn ripped open the plastic bag that held all of Grant's clothing and rifled through it for his wallet and keys.

Got' em! Now I just have to figure out where he left the car.

A quick stop at the nurse's station, and she would be good to go.

"If Mr. Whitley in 112 wakes up before I get back, could you please let him know I just popped out to get some dinner?"

"112? Who's his nurse?"

"I don't know her name," Carolyn said, awkwardly.

"Well, I'll leave a note for his nurse."

"Thank you very much," she smiled "I'd appreciate that."

It is very hard to wait for that (drink, cigarette) milkshake once the jones has set in. Everybody has their addiction.

To Carolyn, the elevator seemed to take at least a

year to reach her floor. Maybe two?

She used the time to think about how nice it would be to sit down and drink a huge milkshake all by herself. She didn't like them once they'd melted, so there was always an ice-cream cough to contend with.

That was okay, too. It was all a part of the charm.

She had reached the lobby and was just pushing through the glass doors to the parking lot when an announcement came over the intercom.

That's funny, Carolyn thought, jiggling Grant's keys. *I could have sworn they just asked for 'Mr. and Mrs. Whitley to please come to the maternity ward...'*

Carolyn chalked the whole thing up to anxiety overload, laughed, and traversed the crosswalk that led to the emergency room parking lot.

There it is! I think I see it next to the red Nissan! Yay! Carolyn cried, inwardly.

Carolyn had been expecting to have a hard time finding it – taking into consideration what kind of a day it had been...

Romancing the (Portal) Stone

Tori collapsed onto her bed and stared around the room. She wanted to cry – needed to cry, but she was still in shock.

Matthew is gone. His lips were touching mine, and everything was magic and wonderment, until his mom showed up and started yelling.

Why didn't he just turn around and come straight back? Tori thought with a heavy heart. *There couldn't have been too many hand placement variations to try. I mean, he knew where he was sitting and how he lost his balance, right? If it was me, I would have come back.*

Of course, Tori knew that it had been an accidental portal flip, so why couldn't she help feeling as though Matthew had left her behind?

Stop it, Tori! You don't know what happened on the other side. He could have been seen coming through, or even landed in something awful and been injured!

If Tori were being honest, what she was really worried about were the other possibilities -- like Matthew being greeted by a sparkly, five-breasted alien with really good hair...

Tori sighed, stretched out on her back and put both hands under her head. It's a whole lot more likely that he was hauled away by a potato posse, and, besides, she knew that Matthew was in love with her. She'd known for weeks. He messaged her things on Facebook that he wouldn't have dared to say to her face.

Tori closed her eyes and remembered the message that had made her tingle for days:

"You always were the prettiest little girl on the block, you know. When we were kids, I used to duck out of sight whenever you went by on your bike with all of that silky brown hair tied up in ponytails and flying wild in the wind."

She had noticed him, too. The shy boy who was three heads taller than anybody else. As Alisha's friend, Tori had spent a lot of time in Matthew's (everybody had called him 'Skink' back then) general vicinity, and had always found his quiet ways to be mature and kind of mysterious.

As Tori grew older, however, she had given up on Matthew Whitley and moved on to the next best candidate.

Matthew was too absorbed in whatever was under the hood of the car that happened to be pulled up in front of his house at the time (and there was always somebody's car sitting out front). As a result, Tori had never even gotten a smile out of him.

That kiss today was something, though. It was slow and tender – the anticipation of his mouth closing in on hers was almost unbearable, and the warmth and softness of his lips when they met had caused her head to fill with a dark, smoky fog that made Tori feel all faint and sensual.

I think a certain Matthew Whitley has fallen in love with me, Tori mused, smiling faintly. *I think I may even have... (Have I?) Yes. I'm sure I've given my heart to the nerdy car guy who lived across the street, and that's just about the most wonderful thing that's ever happened to girl next door.*

It's good to be King

The next thing Matthew did was to flick on the control panel and pull a 360 degree wheelie.

"Whoo Hoo! Here you are, old friend! I swear on a whole box of ice cream sandwiches that I will never go off and leave you stranded again!"

While the sudden movement of the chair had come as quite a shock to the small contingent of Jurrahs in attendance, Matthew's unbridled exuberance had been impossible to resist. One by one, the serious wardens dropped their sour expressions and lit up like so many candles on a cake.

"Oh, you liked that one?" Matthew laughed. "Watch this!"

There was no end to what he could do with that wheelchair. Matthew had spent too many endless, boring days at home since his 'accident' to neglect taking his latest accessory through its paces.

Two wheels, four, figure eights and reverse spirals – he could make that chair dance.

"Some magician has made this human a rare gift," Shakmun observed, drily. "He must be a very important boy, indeed, to employ such a wizard."

"If so, we would not be doing ourselves or the Wise Man of the Agrigars any favors by incurring his wrath," said Brisballah. "I am still in favor of giving this boy his freedom, before we bring the wrath of the entire human race upon our heads."

"If the boy has power and influence, then is he not even more valuable to us?" Nemanic wasn't about to give in to Brisballah's way of thinking. "As long as he is our prisoner, his people will have no hold over us."

Matthew kept up his wild antics with one ear open to their gibberish-filled debate.

I could make a break for it, but I'd only get to the edge of this clearing before my wheels got tangled up in something, Matthew thought, before sighing in defeat. *The terrain is too rough. They'd catch up to me before I'd even gotten free of the trees. What am I going to do? There has to be a way to slow them down, but how? C'mon, Skink old boy! Use your instant noodles.*

Matthew knew that 'The three stooges' (as he liked to think of them) were putting their heads together on the topic of his immediate and long-term future at that very moment.

The chubby one (Brizz something?) was on his side – Matthew felt certain of that – but what the other two had in the works for him was anybody's guess.

Meanwhile, I'm just wasting valuable battery life.

Matthew turned to face his captors and flicked off the power to his chair.

What are they thinking? He would have given anything to know.

"Hey Harry, Curly and Moe, where do we go from here? I'm thinking a stop at Burger King. What d'ya say? A Whopper, large fries and a Diet Coke? I'm thinking they would go down pretty good about now."

The two nasty Jurrah guys turned to consider him -- head to... um... er... stump.

What he saw in their eyes made it clear that, whatever they were planning, it was definitely not something Matthew was going to enjoy.

Matthew gulped.

At the same time, he noticed that the one he knew as 'Brizz-something' did not meet his eye, but had instead moved stealthily to the back of the group and raised... his... axe?

"Axe!" Matthew hollered – partly out of shock – mostly out of sheer stupidity.

Thankfully, by the time the other two Jurrahs had whirled to see what their captive was carrying on about, Brizz's weapon had all but lifted the stuffy one's head from his shoulders and cleaved the weasely one's skull into two equal halves.

Matthew had never seen violence like that outside of a video game, so he cringed into a fetal position on the seat of his chair and covered his face with his arms.

"Don't kill me! Please! I'll do whatever you say! Just don't kill me!"

Hear Ye! Hear Ye!

Grant Whitley, Esquire was happily sipping beef bouillon and watching the 6:00 news when the announcement came over the hospital paging system. "Will Mr. and Mrs. Whitley please meet their party in the 4th floor nursery?" Grant's cup fell from his hand and hit the tray with an explosion of clatter and broth.

"Alisha!"

Everything came back to him in that moment. The phone call, the young man, the emergency Caesarean section...

I have to get out of this bed and find my daughter! What is wrong with me? How could everything have dropped off of my radar like that?

A more understanding voice between Grant's ears was quick to defend the lapse.

You had a fucking myocardial infarction! That's how. They scraped you off the pavement in the parking lot not four hours ago! You really need to start being thankful that you are still among the living, counselor.

Now, stay in bed like a good boy and call your wife to deal with the other stuff.

Grant admitted to himself that doing everything it would take to get him mobile again was too exhausting to think about. Instead, he shuffled through the items on his tray table until he found his cell under a broth-spattered napkin and dialed Carolyn.

Answer your phone, damn it!

Carolyn answered after the third ring, and Grant was stuck wondering how he was going to break this news to her.

"Hey, sleepy-head, did you wake up?"

"Yes. The nurse told me you'd gone to get something to eat."

"How are you feeling? Did they feed you anything?"

"They did. I'm stuck with a liquid diet for the next few days, but, either I was at the point of starvation or it was very tasty."

"Maybe a bit of both," she laughed.

"Where are you?"

"I'm at the hamburger place by the Post Office."

"Ah. Needed a milkshake, did you?"

Carolyn laughed and took another big suck from her oversized straw.

"We've been married too long. I can't get away with anything."

"Honey?"

"That's me."

"I need for you to head back over here right away."

"What's wrong? Has something happened? Are you okay?"

Carolyn's face twisted with sudden concern.

"No. It's not about me." There was a long pause.

Honey?" His eyes dropped to the rumpled sheets of his hospital bed as he fought for the right words.

"What is it, Grant? You're scaring me."

"Well, I think you'd better sit down, if you aren't already."

"I'm sitting! I'm sitting for chrissakes! Tell me what's

the matter."

"It's about our daughter."

"Alisha? What? Have you heard from her? Where is she?"

Carolyn's voice had risen an octave and her words were coming faster.

"Honey, I was on my way to the hospital because I had gotten a call at the office..."

"What? Spit it out, Grant!"

"A young man brought our daughter into the emergency room in pretty bad shape. They were taking her in for..."

"Grant, I swear if you don't tell me I'll have my own heart attack right here."

"Carolyn, Alisha was being taken into surgery for an emergency C-section."

There was silence on the other end of the line.

"Carolyn?"

"What time did that call come in?"

Grant could barely hear the last question as it had come through the cell as a choked whisper.

He hesitated. He had to think about it for a minute before answering. Everything about that day was so blurred by trauma and morphine.

"Grant?"

"I'm here. I'm thinking. My mind lost its grip on all of this when…"

"Yes. Of course it did. Try to remember, if you can."

"The call pulled me out of an 11:00 a.m. meeting, so some time around then."

There was a rustling sound and Carolyn checked the current time on her cell display. It was almost 7:00.

"Oh my God," she said.

"Honey, they just paged us to the 4th floor nursery."

"They did?"

Carolyn remembered the odd page that she had questioned when leaving the hospital. "They did. I think I caught the tail end of it. Convinced myself I was hearing things."

"Well, if there is something to see in the nursery, then…"

"Oh my God," Carolyn said again. "But, what about

Alisha?"

"I don't know, honey, and I can't get out of this room to find out."

"I'm coming now." Carolyn confirmed with a new strength in her tone.

"Carolyn?"

"Yes."

"I think we may be grandparents."

"Ha. I know. I'll be happy about it once I know that everyone is okay."

"Right. Me too."

"I'm on my way. I love you."

"I love you, too. We are going to be alright, you know."

It hadn't been a question.

"Yes. Yes. You stay put and stay as calm as possible, okay? I'll fill you in the moment I've heard anything."

"Thanks. I'll be holding my breath."

"I'm on my way."

"I love you Gramma Carolyn," he quipped.

"Oh my God," she said.

The line went dead and Grant reached for his ice water. Sharing that kind of news on a day like today had been thirsty work.

Murder in the High Trees

Matthew gradually unfurled himself as time passed and no blade had taken any of his available limbs. What he saw when his face emerged from behind his arms was a flushed and bloody Brizz-something-something who was gazing down at the somewhat shorter remains of his two former companions.

"What did you do that for?" Matthew ventured, fully aware that the remaining Jurrah didn't speak his language.

The creature was clearly in shock, and did not make any effort to reply.

"Hey, are you okay, Brizz?"

At Matthew's horrible mutilation of his given name, Brisballah did look up.

"Brizz?" he asked, pointing to himself.

"Yes. Um. Sorry, but I can't remember the rest of your name…"

"Brizz." The gobbet-spattered huntsman said again,

smiling. "Brizz!"

Now, the poor mass murderer (are two gruesome murders enough for a mass?) was laughing as though that was the funniest thing he had ever heard.

"Brizzzzzzzzz!" Brisballah played with the zzs at the end.

The human and the Jurrah both grew silent and stood several feet apart looking at each other.

Matthew pointed at himself and said, "Matthew," again.

"Matthew," repeated the newly-coined Brizz.

Matthew pointed at the two corpses and shrugged his shoulders as if to ask, "What the hell, dude?"

This time he got through and Brizz made an attempt to communicate via a series of hand motions and head shakes that were reasonably informative.

"Ah. They wouldn't listen to you, would they." Matthew had pointed to his ear and then to the dead guys and then to Brizz. "To tell you the truth, I was getting pretty tired of them, myself."

Brizz nodded, seeming to catch Matthew's meaning,

and heaved a heavy sigh before retrieving his gory axe and beginning to scrape the largest bits of hair and flesh off on the trunk of a tree.

Matthew looked away thinking that he should be feeling queasy, and mildly alarmed that he wasn't. Before very long, axe cleaned and ready to go, Brizz spoke again.

"Ex doangu Ghama Traya?"

Matthew thought he understood and answered with an eager nod.

"Yes. The Ghama Traya will take me home. Thank you."

Matthew instructed Brizz to push his chair from behind, which was the best way to get through the heavy undergrowth, and so it was that the two friends journeyed the rest of the way back to the portal in relative peace.

Matthew wondered what would happen to Brizz when news got out about his missing traveling companions. Would Brizz make up a story about what had befallen them? Would he be imprisoned and put to death?

It suddenly occurred to Matthew that this Jurrah had killed for him.

He killed them for me? Why? What does he expect

in return?

Now, Matthew was suspicious. Brizz appeared to be accompanying him safely to the Ghama Traya, or was he? Perhaps, once there, the Jurrah would force him to... but, before Matthew could finish that thought, Brizz had shouldered his axe and begun to sing.

"Itzzy Bitzzy zpi-der climded uppa de waterrr zpout..."

Itsy bitsy spider? Matthew laughed.

Alisha!

Brizz must have heard Alisha teaching some mini-Jurrah-lets how to sing that song – complete with hand motions, no doubt. His sister had always been good with kids. Matthew couldn't imagine that song turning up in this world in any other way.

"Alisha?" he asked over his shoulder.

"Aleeesha," Brizz confirmed.

"Here, let me carry that for you." Matthew pointed at the axe. "Then you'll be able to push this chair in a straight line."

With only the slightest hesitation, Brizz handed

Matthew his weapon and gripped both handles firmly. "Ah!" he said.

"Yeah," Mathew replied, "Now we're cooking with gas!"

"Ooking me Ass!" replied Brizz.

"What he said."

Matthew felt a huge surge of forward motion as Brizz applied the Jurrah equivalent of 'warp speed' to the back of the wheelchair.

I'll Be There

Carolyn Whitley rushed to Baltimore Washington Medical Center just as the day was fading into night. The hilly and curving two-lane road was bordered by trees on either side and Carolyn had to keep switching off her high beams to accommodate oncoming cars.

I'm coming, honey. I'm on my way. Oh my good Lord! Alisha went into surgery over eight hours ago!

Without realizing it, Carolyn pushed down on the gas pedal and increased her speed to ten mph over the limit.

The nursery was paging us, though. The nursery! That means? Well, that means that there is a baby. A baby! I have a grandbaby! Alisha is young, I know, but she has always been mature for her age. Everything will be just fine. But,...

The Lexus was cruising over the top of a hill when

an oncoming pair of headlights required Carolyn to kill her high beams again.

...there has been no word about Alisha. I should have called the hospital! I'm only ten minutes away, now, but I think I'll call, anyway. I need to find out what I can about Alisha and tell somebody that I'm on my way.

Everybody knows that it isn't wise to fool with a cell phone when they're driving. That's why automobile engineers and technicians have put thousands of hours into the development of voice-controlled and hands-free phone management.

It's a safety thing.

Carolyn's car had never been synced with her phone, even though that model had come complete with every bell and whistle, because neither she nor Grant had been able (or willing) to figure out how to set it up.

Now, Carolyn wished that she had just put on her big girl panties and opened the manual. It was dark, and the road was treacherous, but she was a careful driver and she felt certain that she could pull it off.

No big deal, she thought. *I'll just dial information and have them connect me. Surely I can dial three digits without killing myself or anybody else.*

Carolyn laughed at her own hyper-vigilance and freed her right hand from the wheel long enough to dig around in her purse for her cell.

Darn this purse! As soon as I get home, I'm going to throw it out! I can never find anything in it!

That is when Carolyn Whitley took her eyes off the road for just one teensy fraction of a millisecond and hit the deer that had been just outside the ring of her headlights one teensy fraction of a millisecond before.

Absent Without Representation

Rhamas let the Charge nurse lift his daughter out of his arms and place her in a bassinet. There had been no response to the page for Alisha's parents, and it was looking as though they had abandoned their daughter in her time of most-urgent need.

Seeming to read his mind, the nurse said, "I'm sure they are on their way. All kind of things can happen, you know. You would be surprised."

"My Alisha said that her father would bring payment for this hospital."

"Oh, you're not to worry about payment right now. The hospital will take care of your wife and baby for as long as they need it. There is time to think about money after everyone is safe at home."

"I am very wealthy in my country. I hunt large animals for their meat and furs. Will this place accept my meat and furs as payment?"

The charge nurse almost laughed out loud, but bit it back just in time to realize that this strange young man was being sincere.

Where on earth does he come from?

"Please don't worry, I'm sure something can be worked out when the time comes."

"Can you tell me, please, where is my wife?"

"Nurse Lucille promised to call back as soon as she had a room number," she checked her watch. "Wait here for just a minute. I'll call and see if they've made any progress."

Rhamas watched with interest as the kind lady talked into her machine. He knew it was supposed to be a telephone, but it did not look like other ones he had seen. It had square buttons and too many lights.

Soon, his eyes fell on his precious unnamed daughter, sleeping peacefully in her see-through box with wheels. She had lots of dark hair, blue eyes, and full, pouty lips.

"Esmil ka lestin." He whispered above her, which means "Only love for this one," in the language of his people.

"What language is that you're speaking?" The returned charge nurse asked with piqued curiosity.

"It is a tongue of people not of this place," was all the answer that Rhamas cared to give her, and she decided to leave it at that.

"Have you knowledge of my wife?"

"I do. She is in our Intensive Care Unit on the first floor – room 113. Would you like for me to take you there?"

"Yes, most please," said Rhamas.

"Alright," she smiled. "Let me get another nurse to take over here for a few minutes and we'll go up together.

"This is good," Rhamas said, gratefully. "I know that she is sad I am gone from her so long."

While the staffing was being arranged, Rhamas wondered again about what to name his daughter.

The mother of Alisha does not come to the birth of the new hearth child, and therefore does not deserve to take place in the naming ritual.

Rhamas was becoming more and more annoyed with Alisha's parents' and their appalling lack of support.

How am I going to tell her that her mother and father

did not care enough to attend her at this time?

This knowledge will bring my beloved a great sadness, Rhamas knew.

Dream Walking

Alisha felt the sand, cool and wet under her feet. If she curled her toes, they would burrow into it – only to be rinsed clean by the latest wave that danced up and back again. A breeze lifted the hair from her face and put it back down in an arrangement of its own design.

"Alisha?"

A voice called to her as from a great distance and Alisha turned her head to listen.

"I'm here," she called back. "I've always been right here."

A pale blue dress played around her ankles and Alisha tried to remember where it had come from and why she was wearing it.

"Hello?" She called again to the distant echoing dunes that stretched forever into a set of foothills that did not exist.

"I am Alisha. Alisha Lynne Whitley."

As there was no reply, Alisha turned again towards the sea and traced letters into the wet sand with her toe.

"I am here," it declared, briefly – only to be washed away by the gentle lapping of the strangely purple sea upon the shore.

A seagull dipped and swooped above her. It was joined by another, then two more until the evening sky was filled with the sounds of their voices and the flapping of their wings. Their noise and movement brought edges and dimensions to the scene that had been missing before.

Alisha raised her arms above her head and twirled around and around until the iridescent layers of her blue skirt bloomed prettily around her thighs.

Alisha sang out again with exultation as she danced. "I am here and it is beautiful! I am beautiful!"

"Alisha? Please. We need for you to wake up now."

The voices seemed to be calling to her in unison; Male and female, adult and child.

"Child," Alisha repeated aloud, suddenly filled with a sense of unease.

"Who is there?" She called over the roar of the waves and the raucous cawing of the gulls without moving her lips. "Who needs me? Where are you?"

The scene grew suddenly colder. Dark clouds roiled above her, covering the beach in a shroud of darkness that brought Alisha's joyful spinning to an end.

"Alisha? Can you hear me? I am waiting for you to come back, my love. I am here at your side. Can you open your eyes for me? Can you speak to me and give my heart the smallest hope?"

Alisha's heart began to flutter.

Rhamas

I am here, but I should not be here, her dreaming mind argued. *Rhamas needs me, but I don't know how to get back to the hospital. I don't know where to find him.*

Alisha turned her face to the purple sea that had become black and angry with spitting foam. The sky threatened to send bolts of lightning to where she stood, alone on the hard-packed sand.

This is very wrong. There is something I am supposed to do – somewhere I am supposed to be…

"Alisha? Please. We need for you to wake up." Many voices seemed to call to her in unison, now; both male and female – adult and child.

"Child," Alisha repeated aloud.

From somewhere in the distance, Alisha heard the sound of an infant crying.

My daughter! Give me my daughter! She cries out for me! She needs me!

As the memories of her most recent ordeal came flooding back to her, Alisha began to wrestle the borders of the gauzy, dreamlike state she had become encased in. Layers fell away and left her free to swim up and up toward the world of electric lights and beeping monitors that called out so relentlessly to her.

"Rhamas?" It was the faintest whisper through an intubated throat and parched lips, but there had been no reply.

"The baby…"

Though Alisha fought to open her eyes, once she had managed to do it everything was a blur, and there was no Rhamas. No baby.

She was alone.

"Rhamas?" Alisha stirred and made as if to sit up in her bed but the effort was too much for her and she became dizzy and disoriented.

It was easier to drift back to the dream place, where she would be safe and free of pain.

"I will come back when I'm stronger." Alisha whispered to the empty room.

Her lips were cracked and dry, and the tubes that now lived in her nose and throat stole her words before they could have reached anyone's ears, but Alisha knew she had done her best, and that it was time to go.

Alisha's spirit fell away.

Doe, a Deer

The deer rolled over the hood after the briefest thud of impact, and Carolyn could hear the scraping and thumping of its hooves as they scrambled to free themselves of their predicament.

She screamed, then, somewhat after the fact because it had only just occurred to her to do so.

"Oh my God!" Carolyn pulled her car onto the shoulder.

"Oh my God, the poor thing!"

She saw the injured doe laying in the middle of the road and put the car into park.

Should I go over there and see if I can help it? Carolyn thought, wringing her hands.

Should I put on my flashers and hope that somebody stops to help me move her out of the road?

As Carolyn sat worrying over what to do, the doe

somehow managed to struggle to her feet and bound off into the woods on her own.

"Oh my God!" Carolyn grabbed the steering wheel with both hands and rested her head on the bit in between.

"Oh my God! What just happened?"

Carolyn wondered if she might be better off just going straight home and climbing under the covers.

This day couldn't get much worse, she thought. But, even as that crossed her mind, Carolyn knew that she was going to have to get out of the car and survey the damage.

No sense putting it off. With stoic resolve, Mrs. Whitley climbed out of the Lexus and walked around to the front.

That's just great, she thought as she observed the cracked headlights and the crumpled fender with matching hood.

There was a crack in the windshield, but it didn't amount to much. All four tires were still inflated and the creatively-redesigned fenders appeared to have left enough room for their unhindered rotation. All good.

Carolyn heaved a heavy sigh and tried to convince herself that it could have been worse. The fresh evening breeze stroked her face and calmed her nerves, somewhat. It was coming on autumn and the air was cool and fragrant with turning leaves.

With genuine concern she looked for the deer among the trees, and for signs of blood on the road, but found no evidence of either.

Oh, I hope she's going to be okay, she thought. *Poor thing. I should have been paying more attention. She just popped up out of nowhere. I didn't even have time to hit my brakes...*

A pair of distant headlights lit up the pavement where Carolyn was standing and she crossed back over the yellow line to try her luck with the car's ignition.

Please, please, please let it be drivable? She prayed to the God of Wrecked Cars everywhere before even attempting to turn the key.

The Lexus wouldn't start on the first attempt, or the second, but finally cranked and caught on the third go-round.

Carolyn's hands were trembling and she was hesitant to get back on the road so soon after the collision, but visions of her daughter, grandbaby and husband anxiously awaiting her arrival at the hospital spurred her on.

Okay, everybody. I'm coming. Hang in there.

The Lexus crawled along at ten miles under the speed limit with its brights on all the way.

Carolyn didn't think she'd ever take that road at full speed again – not with all of the deer roaming around in the trees on either side just waiting until the right moment to jump in front of her car.

An impatient driver nudged up behind her and flashed his lights, but Carolyn wasn't about to speed up.

"You can just cool your jets, Sherlock." She said aloud to the glare in her rearview mirror. "Don't you know there are all kinds of deer along this road that jump out of nowhere after dark?"

The first honk from his horn made Carolyn jump about a foot. Her hands were shaking, and she worried that she might actually be going into post-collision-stress-syndrome.

"I am so going to road rage all over this dude in a minute," she warned her purse (as nothing else was available at that moment and Carolyn was sure her purse would understand, seeing as how it had been at her side throughout the day's entire parade of mishaps).

After the second and third honk, however, Carolyn pulled meekly off onto the shoulder of the road to allow the jerk to squeal past in a show of burnt rubber and (immature teenage) defiance – albeit while simultaneously praying fervently that his SUV would impact something unexpectedly and tragically only to explode into a million tiny pieces in the very near future.

Carolyn took a deep breath and shoved away her natural tendency to feel guilty about wishing evil (death and dismemberment – *Hell, death by bursting gobbets!*) – on another human being.

Granted, she argued, it was not a nice thing to wish imminent annihilation on a (sub-human Neanderthal jerk-faced-dit-wad) fellow traveler, but, given the full range of retribution at her disposal – it was certainly the most (lame) palatable.

Hold up, she thought, *my inner voices are talking to their inner voices. I need to get a grip.*

With the utmost caution possible, Carolyn Whitley pulled back onto the two-lane highway and proceeded to white-knuckle her way towards the Baltimore Washington Medical Center to bravely confront the next exciting chapter in her very eventful day.

Brisballah and the Stone

With Brizz to push the chair, Matthew's return to the Ghama Traya took half the time. They arrived in good spirits, having thoroughly enjoyed the random bumpiness of the ride (Matthew because it was the first time since the loss of his legs that anyone had felt free to treat him like a 'regular' guy, and Brizz because he got a kick out of making his charge lurch hilariously off in all directions while simultaneously laughing uproariously and hanging on for dear life).

"I'm beginning to think that you mean to kill me, as well," coughed a dusty and red-faced Matthew. "And, just when I was beginning to like your face."

The blood-and-gobbet-spattered Jurrah only nodded, good naturedly, and plopped to the ground to catch his breath.

Both sets of eyes regarded the scarred and pitted surface of the Ghama Traya with reservation.

Matthew hoped his new companion knew the way around the mystical portal, but, when their eyes met, Matthew could tell that Brizz had been hoping the same of him.

"You don't have the slightest notion how to use this, have you, Brizz?"

"Brizz!" the Jurrah huntsman tapped his chest proudly and smiled. "Brizz!"

In the uncomfortable silence that followed, Brizz pointed at Matthew and said, "Mattooo!"

"Yes. Good! Right. I am Matthew."

"Mattooo!"

The dopey exchange brought equally dim-witted chuckles from both guys, which was – of necessity – followed by more uneasy silence and a certain amount of scratching and adjusting of male bits.

Matthew wheeled his chair slowly around the Ghama Traya. He thought he knew just exactly where his hands had been when the portal had launched him to his present location, but that still left the question of what he was going to do with Brizz?

Clearly, the Huntsman had expectations of leaving

this barren world for something more accommodating, but was Matthew ready to take the Jurrah to Maryland? He looked Brizz over from head-to-toe – taking in the leather garments and the knee-high boots. Even if they hadn't been spotted with gore, Matthew knew that the outfit would turn heads in modern-day Odenton.

Where am I going to put you? Matthew thought, grimly. *I can't very well leave you here, can I?* Suddenly, Matthew had an idea. Hadn't the three of them used the word "Agrigar" when they were going on, earlier? It had been one of the only words that Matthew understood. Perhaps he would try it, now.

"Brizz? Agrigar?" Matthew pointed to the large, red rock, before shrugging his shoulders with palms up in the universal pose for "Gimme' a friggin' clue."

Now it was Brizz's turn to circle the Ghama Traya with his brows knit in concentration.

Cool. Now, they were communicating, Matthew thought.

His new best friend was unsure, but did give the impression of having some idea of how to proceed. Perhaps he had seen that stuck-up-now-thoroughly-dead-

and-headless-boss-dude do it? Matthew didn't know. Finally, Brizz had stopped to one side of the stone and pointed at two points about mid-way up.

"Agrigar?" The Jurrah nodded, and shrugged. "Or, close enough for government work." Matthew translated aloud.

I could go with him – you know – just to make sure he made it to somewhere safe... It's the least I could do, seeing as the fellow saved my life.

If Alisha's journal was right, all he would have to do is touch the portal stone in the same two spots to return, where he could (Matthew hoped) then make his own way home.

Maybe, I could just watch Brizz go? Do I really need to escort the guy?

Matthew's eyes met Brizz's and he knew that he would never have peace of mind until he knew – for a fact – that Brizz was safely away from this place.

Matthew knew from reading Alisha's notes that the Jurrahs lived in the mountains of the same world that the Agrigars called home, so getting Brizz to the Agrigar village would be almost as good as taking him to his own front door (sort-of). Matthew sighed and resigned himself to the delay in his homecoming.

He placed one hand on Brizz's arm and nodded towards the stone. Brizz, taking his meaning, positioned himself in front of the portal and indicated for Matthew to take his other arm. The next thing Matthew knew, the two of them were – exactly where they had been one minute ago...

"Craptastic," Matthew said, without enthusiasm.

A Little Help?

Grant Whitley refused his 6:00 p.m. pain meds. He knew that he had to stay alert in order to communicate his dilemma to the (frustratingly) absent nursing staff and find out what was going on with his daughter and grandchild.

Grandchild? Jesus, Joseph and Mary, Grant thought.

When he felt enough discomfort to know he was in his right mind, Grant Whitley pressed the nurse button on his remote control (might as well give it a try), and waited patiently for a response.

"Yes, Mr. Whitley? How can we help you?," came a reasonably friendly voice over the loudspeaker.

"I was just paged to the Maternity floor," he started, "Did you hear the page? My daughter is here having a baby and I would very much like to check her status, please."

"Oh? Well, congratulations, Mr. Whitley. I'll tell your

nurse."

No! No, no, no, no, no! Grant thought, frantically, too politically correct to put his feelings into words over the intercom system.

That's not going to help! You've been doing that since I got here, and I'm pretty sure that there is no such person!

Grant could hear the system click off, and knew that he was going to have to come up with another plan. "Hey!" He called, aloud. "Hey! Is anybody out there?"

He felt absolutely foolish calling for help like some skier trapped by an avalanche, but what else was he going to do?

Grant tried again.

"Hello? I'm Grant Whitley in room 112! My daughter is somewhere in this hospital having a baby, and I need to know how she's doing! Can I get any help in here? Anybody? A little help, please?"

For several tense minutes Grant listened for a response, but got none. He was just about to clear his throat and try again, when a tall, dark, muscle-bound young man showed up in the doorway. His hair was curly, dark brown and shoulder-length. He had the tattoo of a blue compass rose on the cheek under his left eye. The two of them stared at one another with a strange kind of recognition.

"Rhamas?" Grant Whitley asked in a barely-audible whisper, already sure of the answer.

The young man nodded and came forward, hesitantly. "Mr. Whitley," he said in a melodic voice with a heavy accent.

"I look for you very hard, and you are in this place. Are you very sick, now?"

"Alisha?"

"She is here, also. Very sick. Sleeping and not waking. She has borne a girl to be your first hearth child, but there was blood – too much blood."

Grant Whitley dropped his head into his hands and cried. The sobs shook his shoulders and caused pain to bloom anew in his chest and arms.

"A girl. A sweet little girl!"

New Arrivals

Still shaking and probably in the early stages of shock, Carolyn Whitley arrived at the hospital and pulled her car into the parking garage. The somewhat abbreviated front-end of her Lexus nudged itself into a parking space near the elevator on the third floor and she shifted it into park with a suspicious "clunk" sound that hadn't been there before.

Carolyn unclenched her hands from the steering wheel and rubbed the pain free of her fingers. She hadn't realized, until this moment, how tightly she had been gripping the damn thing.

Ouch, she thought as she opened and closed each fist repeatedly.

Carolyn's neck and back were stiff, as well, and her shoulders ached with a dreadful forewarning of what her impending old age was going to feel like – should she ever live long enough to find out.

"Yeah. But, you should see the other guy!" she quipped, hoping that the graceful doe was actually doing better than she was instead of the other way around.

"Lesson learned," she leaned back in her seat and heaved a heavy sigh. "I should have been paying better attention. I was going way too fast. It was my own stupid fault. I know one thing for sure -- I am never going to take that road after dark again as long as I live." Carolyn's thoughts shifted to what still lay ahead. She closed her eyes and tried to calm her breathing and heart rate.

What if my Alisha didn't survive the surgery? Carolyn swept that thought from her mind with an impatient, and painful, shake of her head.

Nobody dies from having a baby anymore. Don't be melodramatic, Carolyn! She's fine, and the baby... The baby? I'm a grandmother? Surely, we wouldn't have been paged to the nursery unless there was a baby...

Her heart leaped and bounced against her ribs with wild abandon at the thought. There was no slowing it down or bringing it under control.

Oh my good Lord! Please let everyone be okay. Please, please. I don't know if I could take any more bad news today. Let me take a healthy grandchild into my arms and feel joy tonight. Give me another chance to tell my daughter that I'm proud of her, and that I love her more than chocolate bars and doughnuts.

Carolyn allowed her eyes to open. She slipped the keys into her purse and took the door handle into her aching fingers and heard it unlatch to free her – once again – from the tomb-like interior of her car.

I'm coming, everybody. Here I am. I'm coming as fast as I can. Mom is on her way to make everything better. Had a bit of trouble on the road, but I'm here now, and here I come. Here I come.

The repetitiveness of the words rang like a mantra in Carolyn's head, and propelled her forward – one step at a time – to face whatever the Lord above had chosen to set before her, and Carolyn Whitley *would* handle whatever awaited her.

That was what mothers did.

The good ones, anyway, she thought.

Whitley? Alisha Lynn?

Carolyn stood at the Baltimore Washington Medical Center's reception desk looking for all the world like she belonged on the hospital's second floor (with all of the other mental patients).

Her hair was standing up in wild points all around her head, and her eyes held that frantic, unhitched look that made a person wonder.

A middle-aged woman with salt-and-pepper hair was working the switchboard. She noticed Carolyn's nervous hovering and held up an index finger to indicate that she'd only be a minute.

While she was waiting, Carolyn noticed her reflection in the elevator doors and began to compulsively pat and finger-comb her hair into submission.

I look like I just jumped out of a plane at 4,000 feet, she thought, wryly.

"Thank you for waiting. How can I help you?"

Carolyn snapped to attention. She had been so obsessed with the reparation of her appearance that she had almost forgotten about the receptionist.

"Yes. Hello. I need to find my daughter. I think she is in maternity."

"Name?"

"Whitley? Alisha Lynn?"

Salt and pepper tapped a few keys and then shook her head.

"No Whitley in maternity."

"Well, she had a baby here today. I know that much. My husband and I were paged to the nursery earlier today."

Salt and pepper pursed her lips and tapped some more keys.

"How are you spelling that?"

"Whitley. W-H-I-T-L-E-Y."

"Nope. No Whitley in maternity. Could she be here under her married name?"

Carolyn flushed scarlet. Alisha's journal had said that she was married, but Carolyn was pretty sure it wasn't the type of union that was likely to show up on any

Maryland court records. Besides, did Rhamas even have a last name? Now, she found herself in the position to do one of two things – first, admit that her daughter was married, but she didn't know her new last name, or second, admit that her daughter was an unwed mother.

Carolyn wasn't one to pass judgment, but she still felt ashamed to answer the woman's question.

"No. I'm sure she didn't register under another name."

"Alright. Let me run her name through our entire directory. Perhaps she is on another floor."

Carolyn waited, anxiously. How much more tension was she going to have to endure? Surely, she had already met today's quota of personal anguish?

"Aha! We actually have two Whitleys in our ICU, and – yes – there she is, Alisha Lynn Whitley, room 113."

The Intensive Care Unit? Room 113? Could Alisha have actually been in the room that was immediately adjacent to her father's? Why was she in the ICU? What was wrong with her? Had something gone wrong with her C-section? What could have happened? Oh my God!

"Oh. Thank you so much for your help! I had no idea!

I need to get up there right away." Carolyn clutched her purse and lunged off towards the queue of elevators.

"Wait! Excuse me, ma'am? Mrs. Whitley?"

Carolyn stopped in her tracks and whirled, impatiently.

"You are going to need this visitor's pass."

"Oh," Carolyn blushed again,

"Yes. Of course. Thank you."

She accepted the ridiculous pastel tag with a clip on one end and rushed off with it still grasped tightly in one hand.

My daughter may be dying upstairs and you want me to give a damn about a little square of paper with a glorified roach clip on the end... Sometimes I think this world has lost its collective mind!

Feeling that she was finally on the home stretch, Carolyn climbed into the elevator and pushed the button for the first floor five times in quick succession – just to show it she meant business.

Matthew's Wild Ride

At first, Matthew had not seen the difference between where he had been on Natalo I and where he was now, on Natalo II. Brizz, however, seeming to recognize his home world with a sense of utmost joy, took the chair firmly under his control and marched Matthew happily along a wide dirt path that had not been evident before.

The fields surrounding the Ghama Traya now had thousands of noticeable shoots thrusting up through the earth as far as the eye could see. The crop had been planted here and was doing well.

I think we made it! Matthew rejoiced.

According to Alisha's journal entries, the Agrigar village must be just ahead and down into the valley below them.

Wow. That was easy. Will it be that simple getting home again? Matthew wondered.

In Brisballah's enthusiasm, Matthew's chair leaped

and rebounded over ruts and gullies along the ancient dirt road, and Matthew found himself laughing while holding on for dear life.

Suddenly, the pitch changed in a dramatic way, and Matthew's chair took off down the hill like a shopping cart over Niagara Falls.

"Help! Brizz! Slow it down! Slow it down!" Matthew called. But, a quick look over his shoulder confirmed his worst fears – Brizz the Jurrah huntsman was no longer in control of the chair at all, but instead was standing midway up the incline and calling wildly after him.

"Matteu! Ist gotins woozle!"

Not knowing what else to do, Matthew did his best to control the chair's path and maintain some sense of balance. He knew that applying the brakes at this speed could prove disastrous, but could not see this hell-bent descent ending well, regardless.

"Matteu! Voys! Voys! D'Agrigars!"

At the only word he recognized, Matthew looked ahead to see a small group of curious creatures standing in the chair's deadly path.

Agrigars?

"No! Get out of the way! I can't control it! You'll get squished! Move! Move out of the way!"

The odd little people had wide eyes that remained unblinking. They wore simple clothing and had vine-like arms and legs. Regardless of the clear danger of his rapid approach, they seemed frozen to the spot, and showed no intention of stepping out of his path to safety.

Finally, with no other option in sight, Matthew steered his chair off the road into a deep ravine full of brambles and other unidentified opportunities for inflicting remarkable bodily harm.

He braced himself for impact.

Though it had seemed to him to happen in slow motion, it was all over quickly.

Matthew lay beneath his overturned wheelchair and struggled for his first breath just long enough to wonder if there would actually be one.

Everything hurt. He could feel blood trickling from his forehead and nose. His hands were like human cacti, bristling with inch-long thorns that burned with alien venom. Matthew raised his head briefly to take in the spike of wood that was buried deeply in his outer thigh. The sight of that last injury was enough to shut him down into a dead faint. Had Matthew been conscious, he would have seen a crowd of curious faces gazing down at him.

Some Agrigar. Some Jurrah. One human and his squear companion, Ahqui.

Prince Charming Awaits?

Tori Chandler couldn't stay away. She tried to convince herself of the futility of her mission, but to no avail.

Matthew was her prince charming, after all, and he was lost in another dimension – perhaps calling out for her at this very moment – perhaps horribly injured and unable to make the return trip without her help. In any case, she wasn't going to just stand by and hope that he could find his way home.

She'd given that idea a good six-hour window before deciding that doing nothing was not going to be an option.

I love you, Matthew Whitley. Tori thought, dreamily. *I am going to find you and make you mine, forever.*

Tori knew that she was mooning like a schoolgirl, but was surprisingly good with that. Apparently, that was what one did when one was hopelessly in love... It was gooey and sickening to bystanders – she knew – but, it was all truth and glory in her heart where it had originated.

Truth and glory and rainbows and church bells and white roses. Matthew's kiss had been the sweetest Tori had ever known. It had left her foggy and entranced – tingly from head to toe and back again. And, then, he had simply vanished!

Where are you, Matthew? Why didn't you just come back to me right away?

Alisha's journal had made portal travel seem infallibly easy. All you had to do in order to return was to put your hands in the same position that had caused your departure.

Tori climbed onto the red boulder and positioned herself where she had last seen Matthew.

He had been sitting right here, She thought, *and, when he kissed me, his hands were right... here... and... here...*

There was no warning. No pop, or whiz, or bang. Tori was her sweetheart's front yard in Odenton, Maryland one minute and NOT the next.

"Matthew?" Tori scanned her surroundings for any sign of him. She saw the fallow fields and the distant forest, but no Matthew.

"Matthew? Are you here? It's Tori! M-A-T-T-H-E-W!"

Tori's voice fell flat on the stubbly dirt of the surrounding fields. Goose bumps came up on her arms and neck that confirmed she was alone in a way that she had never been alone before.

"Natalo I," she said in a whisper. "It's real…"

The Second Son

The elevator let Carolyn Whitley out on the first floor of the Baltimore Washington Medical Center, and she barely spared the nurse's station a glance as she hurried down the hall to ICU Room #112.

As she approached her husband's room, Carolyn thought that she could hear voices and she stopped to listen.

"Rhamas?"

The young man nodded and Carolyn peeked inside to see the handsome young man move towards Grant, hesitantly.

"Mr. Whitley," he said in a melodic voice with a heavy accent.

"I look for you very hard, and you are in this place. Are you very sick, now?"

"Alisha?"

"She is here, also. Very sick. Sleeping and not

waking. She has borne a girl to be your first hearth child, but there was blood – too much blood."

Carolyn entered the room as her husband dropped his head into his hands and began to sob with relief and joy. Without hesitation, she flung her arms around the surprised young man and buried her head in his shoulder and cried as though she had never been happier, sadder, more worried and more distraught in her entire lifetime.

"Rhamas! Rhamas! You are my second son, and I've waited a very long time to meet you and to see my daughter again. Tell me where she is. Where is my Alisha?"

"Mrs. Carolyn? The mother of my wife's hearth? Please, do not cry. She is here. I will take you to her. Right here in this same place where they put the very bad sick."

"Wait! Help me! I want to come with you." It was with much less difficulty that Grant was able to free himself from the hospital bed, as Carolyn was there to assist him with unplugging the I.V. pole from the wall and arranging the plastic tubing into a movable mass. "Is it far?" Grant asked, as soon as he was on his feet.

"It is here. Right here. One room is side to another."

"Is he saying that Alisha is in the next room?"

Carolyn gasped. Even the most serendipitous mind would never have dreamed such a thing possible. But, then again, who could have predicted that – in a single day – her son would be sucked into an alternate universe, her husband would suffer a myocardial infarction, her daughter would undergo an emergency Caesarean section and give birth to a baby girl, and she would drive her Lexus into (what was very likely) Bambi's mother?

So, it was in a daze that the three of them walked next door and entered ICU Room #114 to find Alisha Lynn Whitley, pale, unconscious and on life support.

Then There Were Three

When Matthew regained consciousness, he was bandaged and tucked into a pallet covered in thick furs. The smells that surrounded him were enticing and mouth-watering – some kind of stew, he thought, steaming hot and ready to eat with a thick slice of bread and butter and washed down with a delicious Diet Coke.

"Matteu! En zet Agrigar, anitol. Mu ungler?"

Matthew's eyes focused on Brizz's wide face and dropped to the bowl that he was being offered.

"Yes. I am very hungry. This smells delicious. Thank you."

Of course, for all he knew, Brizz had just asked him if he was ready to die, or if he wanted to wave a chicken over his head, or some other crazy thing that wouldn't make a bit of sense to him, but, given that the stew was being offered at that same moment, Matthew thought he stood a fair percentage of success in translating the

Jurrah's intentions correctly. Matthew struggled to sit up, as he cradled the piping hot bowl in his mummified hands. He was just aching for a taste of the thick concoction.

As he blew on the wooden spoon to cool it, Matthew wondered how long it had been since he had last eaten anything and decided that it had been days. His stomach grumbled and his mouth filled with saliva. The first bite was as delicious as the last scrapings from the bowl. Matthew looked about for something to drink, and was offered a glass of white liquid by a little, dark-haired girl in a beige tunic.

"Milk?" Matthew asked, even though he wasn't expecting an answer. He took an experimental taste of the drink and found it to be milk of some sort – not exactly what he was used to – but not bad. He gulped it down, gratefully, and wiped his mouth on his sleeve.

"Thank you," he said, smiling sweetly at the child. She nodded, took the mug and the empty bowl and walked away without making a sound. Fed and comfortable, Matthew took the time to survey his surroundings.

This must be the Katsan that Alisha wrote about. Just as she had described in her journal, the large building had only one room with a huge fireplace on each end and tables in the center. All around the edges, pallets had been set up for sleeping, similar to the one he was currently resting in. The room was busy with sound and movement, and currently housed no less than forty Jurrah.

Matthew remembered reading that the Katsan served as a sort of hotel for visitors of all races, and that the Agrigar lived elsewhere, in small cottages throughout the village. Alisha had made everything so oddly familiar through her words, that Matthew found himself feeling grateful for the heads-up in – what could have been – a terrifying situation.

At least he knew that the Agrigar were a peaceful people, and that the Jurrah were very accepting of stray humans – as a rule. (Matthew never had figured out what had gotten the huntsmen's panties all tied up in a knot.) Suddenly, a disturbing thought came to his mind.

"Brizz? The Wise Man of the Agrigar?"

Brizz shook his head, emphatically, and smiled. "Nom Wise Man! Morde Wise Man!"

A chorus of laughter went up from all in attendance, and Matthew wondered what he had said that had been so amusing.

"Hello," a female voice greeted Matthew from a nearby table. "The Wise Man of the Agrigar was beaten to within an inch of his life and carried away to the dungeons of Topazial. I doubt that you will ever be troubled by him again."

Matthew's head swiveled to take in this new phenomenon. There was a woman with short brown hair and clothes from his world sitting at a nearby table and enjoying her dinner.

"You speak English?"

"Yes. I'm originally from Wisconsin, actually. My name is Cynthia Lang. Brisballah tells me that you know Alisha Whitley, somehow. Is that true?"

"Cynthia from the Conglomerate?"

The woman's eyes narrowed with suspicion.

"Who told you about the Conglomerate? That isn't supposed to be a matter for common knowledge, as you might suspect."

"Oh. Yes. Um, really? Alisha wrote about you in the journal she left under my pillow. I'm Matthew, um, er, Alisha's brother."

"And, what did she say about us, may I ask?"

"Only that their squear, Ahqui, had originally come from there, and that they had to leave him behind – which broke her heart."

The woman's face relaxed a bit and Matthew decided to be very careful about what he said to Cynthia from that point onward.

"Ahqui! Come here, sweetheart!"

Matthew forgot about any pain he might have been trying to forget a minute before and sat up straight to follow Cynthia's gaze.

Then, he could see the funny creature bounding through the crowded Katsan towards Cynthia in a glory of fluff and unbridled cuteness.

The little squear leapt into the woman's arms and said something that sounded a lot like "What, Momma? What?"

Matthew was floored.

"Ahqui, this is Matthew. He is Alisha's brother, and he has come here looking for Alisha – just like we have."

"Er-lish-errr?" Ahqui said, sniffing the air in

Matthew's general direction, and rotating his little round teddy-bear ears like mini radar dishes.

"Yes. He loves Alisha because she was born from the same mother."

"Ohhhhh," Ahqui's little mouth formed a perfect "O" and he leaned towards Matthew's sleeping pallet to get a better look.

"Go ahead, little one. Go to Matthew. I've got a feeling that you two will be the best of friends very soon."

Anxious to befriend the squear that had captured his imagination from the first time he had appeared in Alisha's prose, Matthew held his arms open wide and welcomed Ahqui to his generously bandaged lap.

The Gingerbread House

Alisha lost hold of her body and fell a very long way. Many odd scenes began to pass her on the way down.

She saw her mother putting the finishing touches on dinner in the kitchen of the home she had grown up in, and she flew past all of the portals she had travelled through on her strange journey.

Once, she had almost managed to catch hold of a massive tree limb from the canopy of Natalo II's dark forest, but the branches had merely brushed through her palms, surrounding her in a shower of yellow, red, and orange autumn leaves, but failing to slow her downward progress in the least.

"I need to get back up there!" she cried aloud, without making a sound. "I have to get back to Rhamas! To my baby! To my life!"

But, the scrolling scenery continued to mock her as she fell past layer upon layer of the life she had lived -- first, with her family, then with her husband.

"This must STOP!" Alisha's mind took a firm hold of the situation at last, and a green ribbon of lawn began gently rolling itself out beneath her feet.

Where am I? She wondered, touching down lightly and looking about for clues.

As the lawn rolled outwards from Alisha in all directions, a landscape popped free of it. There was a little brook, burbling past a charming cottage that was currently nestled within a copse of maple, Oak and Locust trees.

Alisha had never been here before, and it seemed a very pleasant place to be, so she found her way across the brook on conveniently-positioned stepping stones, and followed a newly-lain brick path to the tiny home.

Alisha had barely had time to notice that she was still dressed in a drafty hospital gown, when a simple country dress with a laced bodice and a pair of matching slippers had shown up to make remedy of the matter.

This is a dream, she thought. *I can make everything just as I'd like it to be. It's like my own 'Neverending Story!'*

In order to test her theory, Alisha wished for the tiny cottage to be made out of gingerbread and decorated throughout with assorted candies and glazed sugar icing.

It worked! Lovely! Alisha tried the door and found it unlocked (of course). The smell of warm gingerbread emanated from the large fireplace, and that was shortly joined by the fragrance of pine that had accompanied the sudden manifestation of a floor-to-ceiling Christmas tree with all the trimmings.

Alisha knew that she should be tired and hungry after everything that she'd just been through, but, truth was, Alisha felt just fine! In fact, she didn't think that she would ever need to eat or sleep again.

Why is that thought oddly troubling?

But, Alisha found that distressing feelings were easily dismissed within the confines of a gingerbread house, especially one that was your very own. Besides, there was time to think about more serious matters, lots and lots of time.

A rock-candy chandelier popped into existence in her newly-enlarged foyer, and Alisha smiled.

Tracking Wheels

Tori climbed atop the Ghama Traya and shielded her eyes from the glare of the sun. When looking up and across had yielded her nothing, she cast her eyes to the ground.

There! Tracks! Wheelchair tracks! Plain as day, the tracks wound around the Ghama Traya, then off towards the forest – but, another set came back from the forest, and, this time, Matthew hadn't been alone!

But, nothing lives on Natalo II! Tori argued internally as she dropped to the ground with a grunt and a puff of dust to get a closer look.

And this particular 'nothing' was wearing sandals! Where could he have been heading?

Certainly not home, as he had never arrived.

Alisha and Ahqui used this portal to get to Natalo I and the Agrigar village. Maybe that is where he and his friend (Enemy?) had been going... but, how do I begin to know where the trigger points are?

Tori backed away from the Ghama Traya one full pace, so that she wouldn't disturb any more of Matthew's wheelchair impressions.

Surely, the chair would have had to be facing the stone in order for Matthew to be able to touch it with both hands, right? So, all I need to do is find a place where the chair is facing the...

"Aha!" Tori cried, aloud. "Got it! Got it! Got it!"

Unfortunately, as Tori faced the expanse of available rock surface before her, it was clear that there were still an infinite number of hand placement locations and combinations with which to experiment – and no guarantee that she wouldn't end up in some other dimension, as yet unexplored by Matthew's sister... Maybe an even scarier dimension, with Tori-eating-giant-ten-legged-spiders or some such...

I should go home. Right now. Do not pass go. Do not collect $200.

But, how could she leave Matthew to an unknown fate? What if she was supposed to appear out of nowhere and rescue him like Tonto had done for the Lone Ranger?

Oh, prunes on a Ritz! Tori chided herself. *Surely you can come up with a better duo than that. How old are you, anyway? How about The Joker and Harley Quinn from Suicide Squad, or, or, um, er... Why am I sitting here arguing with myself over sidekick analogies, anyway, when I should be shuffling my few remaining marbles for a next move?*

Tori coaxed the band out of her ponytail and stretched it over her wrist. Then, with her fingers, she massaged her thick hair free wherever it had been pulling against her scalp and sighed with pleasure.

I need to go home, but not without marking where Matthew's wheels faced the portal and not without letting him know that I've been here.

A light came on behind Tori's eyes as an idea presented itself.

She cast about for a stick, found one, and buried it like a fence post with one end poking up dead center between the most-telling set of wheelchair imprints. Once that was tamped in and secure, Tori wrapped her shocking-pink, cloth-covered rubber band securely around the exposed end.

It's like a flame-free flare, Tori mused, standing back to survey the resulting talisman.

If that doesn't do it, nothing will. She thought.

Then, before Tori could talk herself out of doing the right thing and heading back to Odenton, she climbed back up atop the Ghama Traya and did her best to recreate the proper positioning for her return.

Daddy's Here

Grant had availed himself of the only chair in the room and Carolyn had made herself helpful and found an outlet for his I.V. pole assembly.

He was trembling at the sight of his only little girl on life support.

Alisha's dark, wavy hair had been allowed to grow long since he had last seen her. There was a pale blue tattoo high on her right cheekbone that nearly mirrored the positioning of her... (husband's?).

Tubes and wires snaked out of Alisha's bedding and gown and gently-parted lips. Electronic monitors beeped and whirred and sighed all around the room.

She looks like a wax doll, he thought, taking in the pallor of her skin and the sweep of dark lashes that fanned out above each cheek.

Tears began to fall, and Grant made no move to wipe them from his face. He found Carolyn's hand and took it in his.

"She looks like…"

"I know," his wife had been able to read his thoughts for years, so Grant didn't doubt her now.

Together, they watched the young man stroke Alisha's hair and arrange her covers. The weight of sadness that he bore seemed inconsequential in comparison to the love that shone from him towards their daughter.

"She is in a far place where there is much power for healing," he said. "She will return to us when she is ready. I know this. She will not leave her daughter's side for long."

Alisha's daughter… My granddaughter… Grant thought with awe. He started to get up, and Carolyn's hand pushed him gently back.

"Perhaps Rhamas will bring the baby here?" she suggested, questioningly.

"You really aren't in any condition to go traipsing around the hospital – if they'd even allow you to leave the floor."

Rhamas nodded, solemnly.

"The place they keep our child has such laws, too. I have made an alliance with the woman who rules, now. I will ask."

Suddenly unsure about how effective this kid's communication skills would be under the circumstances, Carolyn said, "I think I'll go with Rhamas. Maybe I can help."

While Grant felt a protest rise to his lips, he had to bite it back. Yes. It was unfair that everyone else got to see the baby first, but...

"That's a good idea, honey. I'll stay with Alisha, in case..."

Grant hadn't finished his sentence. Not even in his own mind. Everyone knew how remote the chances were, yet not one person present could bear the thought of Alisha Lynn Whitley waking up, alone.

As soon as they had left the room, Grant spoke aloud to his sleeping daughter.

"Alisha? Honey? Daddy is here. Daddy is with you, and everything is going to be okay. Can you hear me, Alisha? Please try to come back to us. You've already been gone for too long. It's time to come home."

The Face of the Future

Carolyn followed her daughter's husband down the hallway.

'Husband!' I'm going to have to get used to that! She thought, wryly.

"Rhamas? No, honey. The elevators are this way."

One look at his face, however, and Carolyn could see that this was a man who preferred to take the stairs.

"Have you ever ridden in an elevator before?" she asked, gently. He nodded, but seemed hesitant to reply.

"There is no nurse."

"Oh! I can understand how you would think that! The paramedics probably brought you up from the emergency room, and then the nurse came with you to this floor."

The young man blushed and nodded. Carolyn didn't want to make him uncomfortable, so she rushed to make amends.

"That's okay, Rhamas. I would have thought the

same thing! Everybody can use the elevators in the hospital, not just the doctors and nurses. Would you like for me to show you how?"

Then, something astounding happened. Rhamas smiled.

It was a phenomenon! Carolyn had never seen a smile with that much brilliance, warmth and enthusiasm wrapped up inside. It was in that instant that Carolyn Whitley knew what had captured her daughter's heart, mind and soul.

She beamed.

It is humanly impossible not to love this man! Carolyn mused. *My daughter somehow managed to choose the right guy to father her child – no matter what happens...*

"Okay!" Rhamas said, eyes twinkling with the prospect of learning something new and being able to use his favorite Maryland word at the same time. In a few strides they were standing in front of the queue of elevators and Carolyn's lesson began.

"See the arrows on those buttons? One points up, and the other one points down, see?"

Her student looked confused for a moment, probably thinking that those triangles looked like no arrows he'd ever shot from a bow, but Rhamas seemed able to get past that language barrier and he nodded in the affirmative.

"Good!" Carolyn patted Rhamas on the arm for encouragement.

"Now we are going down to the fourth floor where the baby is, right? So, you should push the button that is pointing down."

Rhamas proudly pushed the appropriate "arrow" and then looked at the elevators for any indication that he had activated the doohickey.

"Good! Now, do you see the numbers that are up there -- above the elevator doors? They tell you what floor the elevator is currently on."

"I see the lights," he said, still joyous.

Carolyn's heart fell.

Oh no! What if he doesn't know how to read? Can he even recognize our numbers? What a disaster! I have tried to empower him and only managed to embarrass him further.

Then she heard it. Rhamas was counting along with

the elevator's progress!

"Ten, nine, eight..."

Once again, she was impressed with the man's agile mind. Hadn't Alisha written that he spoke three languages?

When the doors opened and a dozen people spilled out and scattered in different directions, Rhamas looked to Carolyn for further instruction.

"We go in?"

"We do."

"I push the picture of number 4?"

"That's exactly right!"

As the doors slid closed and the elevator car began its descent, Carolyn thought about what the future would hold. Not just for her, and her family, but for a whole world full of people who were about to discover that there were hundreds, thousands, (who knew?) of other dimensions full of discoveries to be made, languages to be learned, alliances to be formed – wars to be fought.

A year ago, I would have laughed at the idea of interdimensional travel. Now – in the space of a day -- her daughter had returned from one world, and her son had disappeared into another! Carolyn smiled at the next idea that struck her mind...

Grant and I always planned to retire to Florida. I wonder if there is a better place out there in the megaverse? Someplace nobody knows about? Just as warm, but maybe not so crowded?

We'll just take a rock to a bench, and then, who knows?

A Real 'Squear'

Matthew had never been much of an "animal" person. His parents had professed allergies to everything with fuzz, and Matthew had always felt that there were better ways to spend his time than scooping poop or dispensing kibble.

Oh, Alisha had whined, made wild promises and cajoled, but – as much as she had longed for a kitten / puppy / unicorn / skunk / raccoon / marmoset / (whatever) – his folks had refused to budge.

In spite of all this, to say that Alisha's squear, Ahqui, was the embodiment of pure joy would have been an understatement.

Ahqui was smart, inquisitive, agile and fluffy.

Who could resist that combination of traits in a squirrel-that-was-a-bear that was a toddler on steroids? Somebody had dressed him in a little green Agrigar tunic, and Matthew could tell that Ahqui found himself extremely handsome in the getup.

"What are you wearing there, Ahqui? Did somebody get you all dressed up this morning?"

The little animal stood up on his hind legs and modeled the new ensemble for Matthew before crouching to leap into his lap.

"Oof!" Matthew exclaimed, still sore in about a million places. "You weigh a ton, little man! No more lasagna for you!"

Completely unconcerned about Matthew's criticism, Ahqui proceeded to pull on Matthew's nose and pat his cheeks.

"He's trying to get you out of bed," Cynthia laughed. "He wants his breakfast."

"Ah. I don't blame him for that," Mathew smiled up at her. "Something sure smells good."

"The Jurrah tribespeople are early risers," she explained, "They eat communally, and breakfast is served."

"I guess I'd better pull what's left of me together and see if I can get to a table."

Matthew shifted the squear to the floor next to his

pallet and lifted the furs away from his legs with some effort.

"Ouch," he complained, "Maybe, I'll just stay put and set my sights for dinner, instead."

"That bad, eh?"

"Let's just say that the wheelchair accident was not the worst of what has happened to me over the last two days."

"Yeah. I was curious about how you ended up with Brisballah and not the rest of his gang."

Matthew's eyes met hers and he wondered how much of the story she could be trusted with.

"Oh, Brizz?"

Christine raised her eyebrows.

He's been great. Really helped me out of a tough situation back there on Natalo II. Don't know what I would have done without him."

"I can imagine," she replied, gathering the impatient Ahqui up into her arms.

"The two jerks he hangs with don't have much use for our kind."

There was a pregnant pause, then she added, "Or should I have said they 'didn't' have?"

Ahqui's whole arm was now pointing towards the hearth fire and the food that was being doled out to all comers.

Matthew gulped. He didn't know what to say to this woman, or how much she knew. Clearly, she had her suspicions that the missing huntsmen were no longer alive.

"Okay, Ahqui! Okay! We're going to get you some breakfast, right now!"

As they moved away, the woman looked over her shoulder and said, "Stay right there, Matthew. We'll bring you something to eat."

Relieved that he wouldn't have to starve, Matthew covered his legs back up and waited to find out what kinds of goodies constituted a Jurrah breakfast. Whatever they were cooking over there, it sure smelled good.

A Whole New Chapter

Tori tried half a dozen combinations of hand placement before she found herself back in the Whitley's front yard. She studied the Ghama Traya, carefully, looking for identifying crevices or colorations that would help her to find her way in the future.

If I mark the stone here in Maryland, will it be visible in Natalo II, as well? Tori wondered.

Of course, leaving road signs like that could open the way for things that don't belong in our world, too.

Tori argued the point internally for another minute or so before lifting her hands from the Ghama Traya and dropping to the lawn.

She wanted to talk to Mrs. Whitley, if only to assure her that she had found Matthew's tracks in Natalo II, and that he had joined up with another human(oid) and probably used the portal to explore a bit further. Also, that he had his chair with him.

I'll tell her that I'm planning to go after him as soon as I've pulled together some camping equipment and supplies, she thought, convincing herself that was true as she climbed into her car and turned the key in the ignition.

Maybe she will want to come with me? I would, if it was my son. Should I offer to take her along? Tori bit her lip.

Of the two of them, (both Mr. and Mrs. Whitley), Tori was sure that Carolyn would be the best asset in a stressful situation. She had shown incredible strength after Matthew's accident; whereas Mr. Whitley had allowed himself to become almost comatose, by comparison.

What am I thinking? How can I even consider taking off into parts unknown without a map – much less with Matthew's mom in tow! Perhaps I am suffering from 'portal lag,' or some such?

Tori switched on the radio and "Jesus Take the Wheel" came blaring out at full volume.

Wow. Maybe I could 'let go, and let God' just this once? I know leaving Matthew out there all alone is not an option...

Why did he go without me?

The question was a nagging one, and Tori wanted to

be furious with him and hurt at the same time.

It only made sense that if she had made it back through the portal after only a few attempts, Matthew could have done so, as well. What could have happened to make him throw good sense to the four winds and take off on his own without food or water or supplies of any kind?

Without me...

Tori's heart kept playing around with that thought as though it was a loose baby tooth – enjoying the pain and the coppery taste of blood – looking forward to the moment that it pulled free.

Determined to shove the cloying doubt from her mind, Tori fumbled through her purse to free her cell.

I've got to call Mrs. Whitley!, she thought. *She deserves to know what is going on as soon as possible.*

Voices in the Walls

Alisha's new home grew and contracted with every vagrant desire. When she had tired of edible gingerbread, the house went Victorian – sporting the architectural kind.

The wrap-around verandah was adorned with swirls and doo-dads – let's not forget the inevitable white porch swing.

There was rosebud and vine wallpaper in the foyer that continued up the sweeping staircase to the first of four landings.

Mom and Dad hate wallpaper. They said it brought the resale value of the house way down because it was hard to remove. I wanted some in my room, but...

Alisha found the thought of her parents vaguely unsettling, and shoved it aside.

They aren't here right now, and this is my house, so I can have whatever I want!

Alisha's little black dog, Misha, jumped into her lap

and licked her face, joyously. Alisha liked that so much that another dog popped into her lap in the blink of an eye; a white one, this time.

Hello, darling? What is your name going to be?

With hardly a pause, Alisha thought how nice it would be to have dogs that matched her wallpaper, and "Poof!" – pink and green dogs replaced the black and white ones and settled in for a warm nap against her spirit body.

Alisha sighed, happily.

A perfect match! She thought.

Then, just as she was really starting to enjoy herself, Alisha thought she heard a voice.

Who could that be?, she wondered, sitting up and suddenly alert.

That voice ... I know that voice ...

One at a time, the little dogs popped out of existence and Alisha listened carefully to seek out the source of the spectral voice. She sat very still, but it did not come again.

Someone was calling my name. I know I heard it! Alisha bit the nails on her right hand and clutched the arm of her rocking chair with the left.

Determined now, Alisha walked out onto her elegant veranda and circled the house with an eye out for any signs of an interloper, but found none. Then, having completed a circuit, she lowered herself happily into the creak-free porch swing and gathered her Persian kittens around her for the comfort of it.

Where did you come from, sweet things? Alisha asked, already knowing the answer.

A pleasant breeze played with her hair and the ribbons on her floor-length gown. Alisha sighed and reveled in the whisper of the leaves as they spoke to her with their gentle rustling.

"Alisha? Honey? Daddy is here."

Alisha's eyes popped open and she sat up – kitties popping out of existence like soap bubbles.

"Daddy? Daddy? Is that you, Daddy?," Alisha called, aloud. "Where are you?" Alisha twirled about wildly in search of her father, but could not see another living soul.

"Daddy is with you, and everything is going to be okay. Can you hear me, Alisha?"

"I can hear you! I can hear you! Where are you, Daddy? I can't find you!" she cried, in desperation.

"Please try to come back to us, will you Alisha? You've already been gone for too long. It is time to come home."

Alisha's spirit face was wet with tears and her arms were wrapped tightly around herself for comfort.

I should not be in this place! I need to go back to the hospital! My Dad and Mom and Rhamas and my... my... baby need me!

The lovely Victorian house disappeared with all of its elegant trimmings, and Alisha found herself standing alone, bare-footed, in a vast forest, wearing only a hospital gown.

Mission Impossible

Rhamas and Mrs. Whitley were still on their way to the fourth floor in an elevator full of people when Carolyn's phone resounded from somewhere deep inside her purse.

Faces were instantly transformed by the ring tone.

Yes. She hadn't had time to change it. *"The Harry Potter Theme."*

As one, the fellow passengers located the offending purse and then raised their eyes to her face with a knowing smirk. It was as if they were all thinking, "Aren't you a bit old for that ring tone?"

Fine. Carolyn thought, ignoring both the ringing phone and the eclectic assemblage's apparent rush to judgment. *But, that book is destined to be a classic!*

To be honest, Carolyn was just glad that she had removed the "Twilight Theme" early last week. (She was 'team Edward').

There had been much said in the news about the hundreds of "lovesick, middle-aged housewives," who had found a way to "revisit their youths vicariously through the characters in a teen romance series."

Okay. Carolyn mused. *That's fair. I fell madly in love with a guy who was less than half my age – and a vampire, besides! So what? It kept me off the streets and curled up in the recliner with a good book. Where's the harm in that?*

She supposed that – given the suspenseful nature of her current lifestyle – she should have chosen the theme from "Mission Impossible."

The elevator stopped on every floor to load and unload doctors, technicians, nurses and visitors. Rhamas seemed to be enjoying himself immensely, but for Carolyn, this was getting old.

She was anxious to meet her granddaughter, and a bit worried about how they were going to wrangle permission to take the newborn up to the ICU.

They had been forced to lie just to get Tori into Grant's room, after all, and there were certainly inherent dangers to a newborn within an intensive care environment that couldn't be denied.

Maybe we shouldn't try to take the baby up there. It could be dangerous. Carolyn thought, as a worry line appeared between her brows.

"My mother. We are on this place we were going."

Carolyn's head whipped up as she realized he was speaking to her. "My mother," he had called her. Well, why not? His mother, she was.

"Yes! This is it! Come along, show me this beautiful baby! I can hardly wait another minute!"

They stepped off the elevator together and there it was – that gorgeous smile of his. Carolyn couldn't help but smile right back, her heart overflowing with joy and gratitude for this handsome young man who had fallen in love with her daughter.

Squear-eyed View

The nice lady named Cineea (Cynthia) always had good food to eat. She wanted to take a trip, and Ahqui enjoyed going places, so Ahqui was happy to go along.

They were his special friends who had found him in the dark forest and brought him home again to be with his family – even though bad men had wanted to hurt him very much.

It was the happiest time when I saw my litter mates again in the glass house! We played and laughed! I was showing Erlisher and Ra-aas my prettiest home and greatest good time joy, but, when I turned around to see her face, Erlisher had many tears on her face! The man pushed Erlisher and Ra-aas out of my glass house and the door was closed tight! Ahqui knew, then, that Erlisher had been sad because the people that kept him in the glass house were making Erlisher and Ra-aas go away and leave him behind.

When Cineea said that she wanted to find his Erlisher (Alisha), Ahqui was even happier, because he missed Erlisher and Ra-aas (Rhamas) very much and wanted to find them, too, but he didn't know where to look.

Then, Cineea showed Marreuu (Matthew) to Ahqui, who he thinks must be Erlisher's litter mate, but he can't be sure because he doesn't understand people words except for 'same' and 'mother,' which Cineea said about Marreuu. He is a man with no legs or feet and he has many hurts on his body. Ahqui wonders what happened to make Marreuu that way, and knows it must have been very bad.

Cineea said that Marreuu would be my 'very good friend,' which I know what that means, and I will be best for him because he needs help getting things out of reach and I know that trick the best of all! Ahqui thought, with pride.

We will find Erlisher and Ra-aas together, and that will make us all happy. They are not in this place. We must go other places to find them.

Ahqui took the plate of hot food that Cineea gave him and carried it across the Katsan to Erlisher's litter mate.

I will have to make Marreuu much better, first. Ahqui balanced the plate of food very carefully as he pounced unceremoniously onto Matthew Whitley's sore middle.

"Ooof!" Matthew had said, then, "Oh. Thank you, Ahqui. This looks very tasty!"

Ahqui thought it looked tasty, too. He stared pointedly at a piece of crispy meat until Marreuu picked it up and offered it to him.

"Here. Do you want to try that piece?"

Ahqui took the meat and nodded, distractedly, as he chewed.

One Story to Go, Please

Tori was not thrilled to see her mother's car in the driveway when she pulled up to the house.

Oh jeez. What am I going to tell Mom and Dad? She thought. *I never go camping by myself! They know how much I hate the great outdoors!*

Not knowing what else to do, Tori just let herself in the front door and called out her usual greeting: "Heyo, Mom! I'm home!"

"Hi, Sweetheart! Where have you been all afternoon? Isn't today your short day?"

Mrs. Chandler came out of the kitchen drying her hands on a dish towel.

"Oh. Here and there," Tori replied, setting her keys in a dish by the door. "I love this kind of weather! No gnats or mosquitoes."

"It's getting cool out, though," her mother warned.

"You really should start wearing a jacket, or at least something with sleeves. You don't want to get bronchitis again."

"You know what I read somewhere? Bronchitis isn't caused by cold weather, at all. It is just a virus that you pick up from other people who don't wash their hands enough when they are sick. Same for the common cold."

"Uh huh. Tell that to somebody else's mother, Tori. You get sick every single year at about this time, and you have done for as long as I've been your mother – which is, from your standpoint – forever."

"Okay. I guess I'll have to defer to your wisdom and break out the winter wardrobe." Tori crossed to her mother and gave her a hug and a kiss on the cheek.

"Tori! You're filthy! How did your hands and feet get all covered in red dust? Look! You've tracked it right through the living room!"

"Oops! Sorry, Mom. I was helping Matthew do some yard work for his mother, and…"

"That's nice, Honey. Maybe you can talk Matthew into doing some yard work over here next time? I'd like to buy some Mums and plant them along the front walk, but I can't imagine when I'll find the time."

"I'm sure he would be happy..." Tori started.

"Please take those shoes off and leave them on the porch, will you? Then, wash up and change. I could use some help getting dinner on the table tonight, and I'm going to have to run the vacuum, now on top of everything else."

"No prob." Tori chirped, brightly. She was glad for any excuse to leave the room and start pulling things together for her trip. "Be right back!"

Tori had no idea when she would be leaving, or for how long she would be gone – only that she wasn't coming home without Matthew. She peeled off her clothes and stepped into the hot shower with a sense of relief.

This feels so good, she thought, *who knows when I'll get another hot shower?*

That was one of the things that Alisha had neglected to write about. Neither bathing nor toilet arrangements had made it into her detailed journal entries.

I doubt very much that the Jurrah tribe had indoor plumbing, she conjectured, wrinkling her nose at the prospect of having to use a communal hole in the ground, or something equally primitive.

What am I going to tell my folks! I can't just 'vanish' the way Alisha did. I'm only taking a partial class load at the community college... could I convince them that I was on some kind of class trip for extra credit?

Tori lathered her hair for a second time and let the suds and hot rinse water cascade over her face, chest and back instead of her usual hair-only rinse. She wished that she could temporarily disappear into the cascading water where none of these distressing thoughts could follow.

If I was a parent, I wouldn't fall for a story like that.

But would her parents believe it? They might. They led busy lives – always rushing about. Tori considered the story from all angles as she applied the crème rinse to her hair and shaved her legs. By the time she had stepped out of the shower and wrapped herself up in a towel, she was fairly certain that she could make everything work out just fine.

And, besides, they trust me, Tori said to the steamed-up mirror as she combed out her hair.

New Beginnings

Carolyn thought that she might pass out as they approached the maternity ward nursery window until she realized that she had been holding her breath from the moment that she and Rhamas had stepped off the elevator onto the fourth floor.

Breathe! She reminded herself, sternly. *If you don't, they'll have three Whitleys on their 'guest' registry!*

As they got closer, Rhamas took the lead. Carolyn could see that he was anxious to show off his daughter for the first time, so she hung back a few steps to allow him to make the 'big reveal' he'd been longing for.

Rhamas walked into the nursery with all of the confidence of a staff member, leaving Mrs. Whitley at the viewing window with a dancing heartbeat and tear-filled eyes – one palm pressed to the glass.

There were at least eight bassinets with wriggling miracles inside. The newborns were all swaddled in flannel blankets of striped pink or blue contrasted with the whitest of whites. Some had shocks of black hair and others were rocking a headful of pale fuzz or the beginnings of a new afro.

Do they always have this many babies? Carolyn wondered if there had been a full moon. Hadn't somebody told her that there were more babies born during nights when the moon was full?

A matronly nurse crossed to greet Rhamas as though he was a returning son, rather than just one of the dozen or so new daddies that must be clamoring for her attention.

Carolyn understood the woman's reaction to the young man. There was something so childlike about him, and then there was that dazzling smile…

While the two of them were conversing, Carolyn perused the tiny faces on display – hoping to be able to tell which pinkly-wrapped bundle belonged to her. It was impossible to tell the infants one from another.

Growing increasingly impatient, Carolyn Whitley gave in to her impulses and tapped lightly on the window until the head nurse and Rhamas turned to acknowledge her.

Having gained their attention, Carolyn waved and smiled sweetly as if to say, "Hello! I'm the new Grandma! I'm about to burst over here! Let's get this show on the road? What d'ya' say?"

To her delight, the nurse flashed a smile and waved for Carolyn to join them inside.

Carolyn's heart was fluttering alarmingly as she moved towards Rhamas. She had wanted to hold a grandbaby before she'd even given birth to her first child! To have this blessing thrust upon her from out of the heavens with no advance warning had been a shock, to say the least.

Carolyn knew that there were tears in her eyes and that her hands were trembling horribly. Rhamas, seeming to understand her barely-controlled rush of emotion, moved to offer his hand and bring her the rest of the way to the baby's bassinet.

The young man's face was full of a mix of pride and empathy as he carefully scooped up his little girl – as yet, unnamed -- and presented the infant to her grandmother for the very first time.

A Star is Born!

With the care of Brisballah, Cynthia and the mischievous, (eternally-ravenous) squear, Matthew's body began to heal. Though he no longer had the photograph of Alisha to show around, Cynthia had known enough Jurrah and Agrigar to circulate the truth of his identity among the villagers and the current residents of the Katsan.

Alisha and her husband, Rhamas, had been well-loved among the people, and many felt bad about having caved to the threats of the Wise Man and the Jurrah huntsmen that had insisted on their arrest and ultimate flight from Natalo I.

There was much curiosity as to what had happened to rob Matthew of his legs, and what better opportunity to regale his new friends with the terrifying tale of his life and death struggle with a monster of the sea!

A crowd formed to listen as Matthew described the beauty of Hawaii and the wonder of the great oceans and some of the miraculous creatures that lived in them.

Matthew had never been much of a talker, much less a storyteller, but he found himself warming to the role almost instantly.

"And, there is a fish in the ocean that is bigger than four of you placed end-to-end!" he said, "It has a mouth full of sharp teeth that can swallow a man whole, and can open as wide as the mouth of that barrel..." As a dramatic finish to his story, Matthew raised up his shirt to display the scars left by the tentative bite of the great white shark across his back and abdomen, following by exposing the ugly stumps that the beast had left behind. This had been followed by a gratifying hush among all assembled.

Needless to say, Matthew was becoming quite the celebrity. Nothing like this had ever happened to him before, and he thought he might easily come to get used to the attention.

The first time Matthew had powered up his chair, the awe that the gadget inspired had been amazing, and Matthew had to admit that he hadn't minded being the center of their universe for however long he could manage it.

For the better part of an hour, he took the chair

through all its paces, doing wheelies and rolling up onto one while the other spun uselessly in midair. He gave rides to anybody who dared, and even let a few of the braver candidates work the controls for a bit.

This is more like it! Matthew thought, laughing to himself. *I could enjoy living here! No wonder Alisha had seriously considered making Natalo I her permanent home.* He knew that there was a lot more of this world to see than Alisha had been able to explore, too.

Clearly, the Jurrah lived somewhere among the mountain peaks that could be seen off in the distance. Matthew wondered whether or not the visiting Jurrah would be willing to take him along when they set out of their homes over the next few days? The thought made a thrill of excitement rise up through his middle like a ride on a particularly wild roller-coaster.

Just as quickly as the dream bubble had formed in his head, a reality pin came out of nowhere to burst it.

Tori.

The thought of her at home, worrying and waiting for him to return brought Matthew right back down to earth with a "SMAT!"

I can't just leave her behind. Not now. Not with things the way they are between us.

The memory of her tender kiss filled him with a longing to go home again.

Maybe, the two of us could make a life here? Who knows? My whole family might consider putting down some roots with the Agrigars?

Matthew laughed at his unintended pun. *Well, it's not out of the 'realm' of possibility, right?* He thought, cracking himself up with his own 'shitty-wittery.'

Matthew announced that he was getting tired, and that the 'show' was 'over for today.' Cynthia obediently translated his message to an extremely disappointed crowd of Agrigars and Jurrahs, both young and old, though nobody exhibited any true signs of resentment.

He was a star! An interdimensional sensation!

But, Matthew was tired – big-time tired – and, it was almost dinner time…

Long Time, No See

"What are you doing in here, um, Mr...., um...?" a uniformed woman that Grant had never laid eyes on was standing in the doorway with a hand on her hip.

"Grant Whitley. Room 112." Grant supplied, clearly irritated.

"You are not supposed to be in here, Mr. Whitley. Your room is next door. As a matter of fact, you are not supposed to be out of your bed."

"Ah. I got lonely in there. Haven't seen a staff member in several hours. Thought I would keep this young lady company. She might need a drink of water or something, you know? A trip to the toilet? A change of clothes or bedding? One of those 'general patient care' type of things that is supposed to happen in the hospital."

The nurse – who was too dark in her complexion to actually blush – showed every indication of being mortified.

"I have just started my shift, Mr. Whitley. You should

know that you are not alone in your feelings. I'm afraid we have had a bit of a personnel shake-up today, and several of our nurses just up and walked out."

"Oh! Well, I'm sorry to hear that. Still, that sad story doesn't wrestle me out of a vomit-soaked gown, or get me a sip of water, or help me get to the toilet in one piece, now, does it?" he said, still hanging on to his well-earned inner curmudgeon.

Her eyes fixed on some invisible spot near her feet, and Grant started to feel sorry for her. Grant wondered how old she was, and decided she couldn't be older than 25 or 26. He couldn't read her ID tag, and still didn't even know who he was talking to.

"I agree. There's just no excuse for it, Mr. Whitley. All I can do is promise that you will have excellent care while I am on duty. You are also free to contact our patient advocate. Her extension is displayed on the dry-erase board in your room – which is room 112, not 113. Let's start by getting you back where you belong, okay?"

"No. That is not okay. You see, this young lady is my daughter. She is fighting for her life, and I have no intention of leaving her side. Not for a minute."

"Mr. Whitley, I'm sorry about your daughter. I didn't know. What you need to understand is that you are *both* here fighting for your lives. You are very ill in your own right. I'm going to have to insist that you get back into your bed."

"Nurse... I'm sorry, what's your name?" Grant strained to see her ID.

"My name is Nurse Timmons. Please just call me Addie."

"Okay, Addie, wouldn't it be possible to move my bed and all of those gadgets in here? I won't rest a second if I'm worrying about my baby. Surely, you can make the powers-that-be understand that?"

Addie's face crinkled up with consternation.

"Listen, if the old sympathy-empathy-heart-warming thing doesn't get it done, how about pointing out that I am a high-profile-nail-your-ass-lawyer who has a great deal to say about any hospital that does not provide me with the bare minimum of care in their goddamned *Intensive Care Unit*? Think that would add any weight to my request?"

"I'll make a deal with you, Mr. Whitley," Addie gave him a crooked smile. "You go get into your bed and let me hook up your leads and monitors, etc., and I'll go see what I can do about making this a double room. Deal?"

"You drive a hard bargain," Grant laughed. "Okay. You're going to have to help me, though, I can't get out of here under my own steam."

The nurse called "Addie" smiled at Grant and reached way down behind Alisha's bed to unplug his IV pole apparatus, then looped the cord loosely over the monitor and offered him an arm.

"Alley Oop!" she said, as he strained to stand.

"Hey," he protested, mildly, "wouldn't that be 'Addie-Ooop' in this instance?

"Sure." Addie rolled her eyes and smiled, good naturedly. "Whatever you say, Mr. Whitley. Whatever you say."

Abandoned Treasures

Cynthia guided Matthew's wheelchair across the town commons and up to the entrance of a walled courtyard belonging to the ex-Wise Man of the Agrigar. The remains of a formal garden withered in place around an arrangement of wildly-colored stepping stones that seemed to swirl off in every direction, creating an awe-inspiring display of wealth and magical intentions.

They followed a path to the front door, which was very large and brightly painted with a mix of royal purples and azure blues. Oddly, for Matthew, the grand entry had been left standing slightly ajar.

"What the hell?" Matthew started to ask.

"Goat-eyed soldiers covered in blue tattoos came from some world called 'Topazial' and took the Wise Man into custody," Cynthia explained, struggling to get Matthew's chair across the threshold. "Nobody in the village knows how the Wise Man could have committed an act of treason without ever having left the village, but that's what he was being charged with."

"Wow. Alisha wrote that he was some kind of a great wizard with terrible powers," said Matthew, confused. "How did the goat dudes manage to arrest him in the first place?"

Then, before Cynthia could begin to answer his question, Matthew was assaulted with the vilest assortment of odors that had ever attempted to traverse his nose hairs.

"Oh, Good Merciful God in Heaven!" he exclaimed, slapping his hand over his nose and mouth and trying to breathe through his ears, instead. "Who gutted the warthog, basted it in green baby bat shit and left it in the oven at 275 degrees for about a year and two days?"

"Come on, Matthew. It's not that bad," Cynthia said, gagging a bit, but impressed with his snappy and on-point verbal assessment.

"Really?" Matthew released his face and attempted to breathe normally. "And, I'm guessing that you can't detect the soupcon of the aroma common to the dirt-from-the-grave-of-a-300-pound-maggot-infested salmon, either?"

"Okay. It reeks in here," she allowed. "Come on, let's look around and then we can leave! The Agrigar tribespeople say that there are vast riches in this house, but everybody is too afraid of the old guy to touch anything."

Matthew thought about the kind of life he'd be able to give Tori with even a tiny portion of a wizard's treasure, and nodded.

"So? How did the guards take him down?" Matthew asked again, truly curious.

"Well, the Agrigars who worked for the Wise Man said that the blue soldiers just walked in and started beating him over the head with clubs until his skull caved in."

"That would do it." Matthew observed. "I wonder why nobody ever thought of doing that before?"

Cynthia laughed and shook her head at the kid. "I guess everybody figured he would turn them into a frog or something. These guys didn't know anything about the man, other than the fact that they were supposed to drag him off to some dungeon somewhere."

"Stupidity is a powerful thing." Matthew observed, wryly.

"So it is!" Cynthia answered, adding, "Let's get this over with, what do you say?"

"You're driving." Matthew replied, clearly willing to proceed.

The foyer led to a formal living room on the right and a shambles of a dining room to the left.

"Great. He was one of those hoarder-types like they have on TLC," Matthew observed.

Cynthia lived in a reality that didn't have Verizon Fios or cable TV, so she had no idea what the kid was talking about, but moved his chair into the more-spacious living room for a look around.

Unlike all of the other houses in the village, the wizard's house was carpeted wall to wall in royal purple and accented with detailed hand-knotted Persian rugs. The main focus of the room was a very large, high-backed chair with ornately-carved mahogany arms and legs.

"This must be the guy's throne," Matthew said, "Alisha said that he greeted all of his visitors from atop that thing."

"Hmm. If he was as tall as all of the other Agrigars, he probably needed a ladder to climb into it," Cynthia said, and they both snickered past pinched noses.

"Wonder what's in the desk?" Matthew switched on his chair and drove it across the room to investigate while Cynthia, interested in picking through some of the piles in the adjacent dining room, drifted off in another direction.

The Wise Man's home wasn't particularly large by Maryland standards, but it was stuffed to the brim with interesting items: So much so, that Cynthia and Matthew didn't cross the threshold again until the sun on Natalo I had begun its slow descent to the horizon.

Each explorer came away from the abandoned home with a bag (or a basket, in Cynthia's case) of semi-precious items to be examined at a later time and in the light of day.

Matthew pulled the front door closed until it latched as he left, fully expecting the Wise Man of the Agrigar never to return and come looking for the people who had robbed him of his most precious possessions.

On the very top of Matthew's pile of stolen booty, there lay a dog-eared, leather-bound volume entitled the "Otherworld Gateway Atlas."

The Wall of Relics

Alisha stood alone in the forest for a long time, knowing where she needed to go, but having no idea how to get there. She gazed at the tree canopy hundreds of feet above her head and considered the complete lack of handholds on the massive trunks.

Clearly, "up" wasn't going to be an easy direction to go, and "up" where she stood was not going to get her back to where her body was waiting in the lonely hospital room. So, Alisha picked a direction at random and started walking.

Patches of sunlight caressed her face wherever the leaves allowed it to pass. Twigs snapped under her bare feet, but they could have been feathers for all the pain they caused her. The sound of rushing water refreshed Alisha's uneasy heart and blessed her passage with tiny droplets and cool breezes.

"I am coming back, Daddy," Alisha said aloud to the music of gently rustling leaves. "I will be there soon, just wait for me. It is a long way, but I heard you calling, and I am coming."

A magic elevator or a flying unicorn would have been more helpful, really, but those things were not present in Alisha's fragile world. Her path was instead ordained by the inner workings of a troubled mind, and it was destined to be an arduous one – full of dangers and hardships – as Alisha had fallen a very long way to get where she stood, and would have to climb a similar distance to return.

It all made perfect sense, sort-of...

Alisha walked on until she came to a place where the vegetation formed an impenetrable wall. She parted the heavy vines to find that they were obscuring a vertical cliff face that rose so high above her that it seemed to disappear within the clouds in a steadily darkening sky.

"This is the way up," Alisha said, relieved to have found it, at last. "All I have to do is climb to the top, and get back into my body. I'm a very good climber, so it won't take long at all."

As Alisha watched, strange items began to push their way out of the cliff face. She was grateful for these, as they would provide safe places to support her hands and feet during her perilous ascent.

The first items she grasped were the back ends of the brave flip-flops that had accompanied her on the journey through the never-ending corn maze and into the portal to Natalo II. The next object she grasped was the pouch that held the fire starters – Ahqui's first gift to her at the campsite in the deep forest.

One after another, the relics of her adventurous past seemed to grow from the stone like a ladder for her to climb safely upward. The beaded white moccasins from her wedding ensemble, the precious wedding gifts of pottery, fine furs and ornaments for her hair.

Each memory had encased itself in stone in order to support her weight, and every one of them brought Alisha great joy in the remembering of them.

Higher and higher she climbed, never seeming to get anywhere but up, just pushing onward through the relics of her now-distant past. There was a thick shard from a blue glass highway, a crystalline plate and bowl used by Xiri to serve fishes and small fowl.

With each item came a rush of sights and sounds long forgotten, and tears began to wet Alisha's cheeks.

They were not the tears of grief or loss, but only the gentle reminders of the beauty she had been allowed to see and the friends that she had been blessed to know.

A handful of gemstones from the sea below Topazial, and the handlebars of -- first Alisha's bike and then Rhamas's -- soon emerged. The fresh smells of cinnamon and ginger that surrounded the jeweled mountain she had so recently called home pervaded the air around her.

I'm getting close, now. Alisha thought. *It can't be much further. I've nearly run out of memories to hold onto!*

And then, as though from a great distance, Alisha could hear the echo of a beeping monitor and the rhythmic hiss of a respirator and she knew that she was almost home.

Where's Everybody?

Grant Whitley settled into room 113 and kept his eyes on his precious Alisha in the next bed over. The hospital administration had opted to take the less litigious road and allow him to have his way.

"That's as it should be," he had said to anyone who would listen – from the techs who shifted all of his monitors to the orderlies who wheeled him and his bed into Alisha's hospital room. "I am her father, after all, and there is no way I could possibly be expected to relax and recover while she was lingering near death in the next room!"

The whole transition had taken place in less than an hour, and Grant had no complaints (at the moment) about either the process of approval or execution of the move. It was only as he was finally alone with Alisha that Grant had begun to wonder what had happened to his wife and the young man that had gotten his daughter into this mess in the first place.

Where is everybody? He thought. *Surely, it can't take that long to get a baby from the fourth floor to the first? Maybe they are having trouble bypassing the regulatory requirements of the hospital's nursery? I don't suppose they are asked to release babies to ICU every day of the week...* Grant scratched his head with his only free hand.

Now that Grant was thinking about it, where had his son been throughout all of the day's confusion? Carolyn hadn't so much as mentioned Matthew's name, and he knew that his son would not have wanted to be left out in a situation like this.

Matthew had missed his sister as much as the rest of them, maybe more, and Grant knew that his son would not have wanted to leave his father alone at a time like this.

Carolyn hadn't even mentioned Matthew. She hadn't nervously dialed his cell repeatedly, or fussed and fumed about why he hadn't gotten a ride to the hospital. Come to think of it why hadn't she brought Matthew with her in the first place? She had come with Tori. These days, one rarely saw Tori without Matthew or visa versa.

Something was wrong.

The thought caused a series of bubbles to travel up

Grant's esophagus and pop halfway to the top, filling his chest and throat with a sheet of corrosive acid.

Grant fumbled for the remote control that was dangling from his bed rail and found the "Nurse" button.

"Can I help you?" said a disembodied voice from the nurse's station somewhere down the hall.

"Yes. Could you ask Nurse Timmons to bring me an antacid and a glass of water, please? Also, when can I get more pain medicine?"

"I'll ask her to stop in," the voice promised with every indication of politeness.

"Thank you," Grant replied, thinking that he'd believe it when he saw it – in spite of himself.

When Addie gets here, I think I'll have her call up to maternity and find out what's what. Surely, Carolyn and this Rhamas character won't be much longer, then, maybe I can find out what's going on with my son.

What are they keeping from me? Grant worried.

Dear God, tell me there isn't some other disaster that I'm destined to find out about before this day is through.

Dire possibilities flashed into focus behind Grant's

eyes. Could Matthew have been involved in an automobile accident? He was always riding off into the sunset with those friends of his – the ones that Grant didn't wholly approve of. Could one of them have run a red light or been t-boned with Matthew in the car? Whatever it was, Grant knew that it must have been a doozy for Carolyn to have been so closed-lip about it.

Well, no more! He thought. *I'm going to find out what's going on as soon as my wife sets foot into this room!*

More acid bubbled up at the thought and Grant felt as though he was going to throw up.

Where's Addie? Grant thought, feeling afraid and decidedly unsettled. *Where are Carolyn, and Matthew? Where is everybody?*

A sharp pain clutched at Grant's arm, back and chest in a relentless spasm. His ears filled with the cannonball booming of his strangled heartbeat as it desperately vied for attention.

Grant Whitley, Esq. fumbled for the remote and mashed all of the buttons frantically with an unresponsive hand – then, like a puppet with severed strings, he slumped over the bed rail and dangled there to the music of multiple beeps and alarms that he would never hear.

A small voice came from the opposite bed that nobody was there to hear. It called to the image of a man that stood over her upon waking -- a man who smiled lovingly and stroked her hair – a man who wasn't precisely alive.

"Daddy? Daddy? Is that you?"

First Contact

After several frustrating attempts to reach Mrs. Whitley, Tori was thrilled to finally get Carolyn's voice on the other end of the phone line.

"Hello?"

"Mrs. Whitley?"

"Tori?"

"Yes! Gee. Where have you been? I've been trying to reach you for the last three hours!"

Tori stood up from her bed and started to pace the room. Her open backpack was already partially packed for a return trip to wherever it was that Matthew had gone.

"Well," Carolyn smiled down at the cherubic bundle in front of her. "We've had a couple of interesting developments over here."

So have I, Tori rolled her eyes, *if she only knew!*

"Oh, no. What's going on? Is Mr. Whitley okay?"

"Yes, yes, he's fine." The red-faced infant wriggled a bit in Carolyn's lap and made a mild protest that sounded a lot like a kitten's plaintive "Mew!" She juggled the phone a bit before continuing.

"What was that?" Tori asked, "Where are you?"

"I'm still at the hospital. You aren't going to believe this," Carolyn said, "but that other Whitley that came through the Emergency room earlier today was our Alisha!"

"What? Oh my God! Alisha? So, she's back? Was she hurt? Is she okay?"

"It's a long story."

"Jeez! Remember who you're talking to, I think I'm beyond shock and awe about anything you could possibly tell me. Besides, I've got nothing but time. What's going on over there?"

Sitting deep within an overstuffed glider in the hospital's nursery, Carolyn Whitley exchanged looks with the handsome Jurrah that was reaching down to relieve her of the increasingly-antsy baby.

"I know! Why don't you come here and we'll tell you all about it." Carolyn's eyes glittered with the prospect of revealing such a glorious surprise.

"There are a couple of people here that I'd like for you to meet! Please, we'll meet you near the elevators on the fourth floor. Okay? I promise it will be worth the trip."

Tori looked at her watch with impatience. It was just after three in the afternoon. The hospital was not where she had anticipated spending the rest of her day, but she desperately needed to tell Matthew's mom what she had seen on the other side of the portal.

"Okay. Are you sure you can't just tell me over the phone?"

"Nope. Just trust me. This is not something you are going to want to miss."

Tori gave her reflection a shrug and a sigh. This was – after all – the woman who might someday (God be willing) be her mother-in-law. Besides, maybe Alisha could tell her where Matthew might have gone and how to get there?

"Well, I guess I can do that. Is there anything Mr. Whitley or Alisha need that I could bring along?"

"Nope. Thanks, hon. You are a star. Just come straight over and we'll be waiting for you."

Tori shoved some remaining items into her backpack and stowed it in her closet behind some boots.

Her parents weren't the snooping type, but it never hurt to be careful.

"Mrs. Whitley asked me to bring some things over to them at the hospital, Mom. Save me a plate, can't say when I'll be back."

"Okay. I guess it can't be helped. Please tell them I'm sorry about what happened, and ask if there's anything I can do."

"Okay! Thanks, Mom. See you later."

Tori slipped on some flats and grabbed her purse and keys.

"And wear a jacket!" Her mother's voice shrilled from across the house.

Tori had barely slipped behind the wheel and put the keys in the ignition when her phone rang.

"What, now?" She whined, exasperatedly.

A Basket full of Squear

Matthew greeted the new day full of purpose and direction. He felt better, and was ready to make the trip back home before his family could drop dead from worry over his whereabouts. Ahqui waddled over to Matthew's sleeping pallet juggling a bowl full of bread, fruit and rosungi (the Jurrah equivalent of bacon) and plopped down at his side to partake of the bounty.

"Heyo, little cowboy," he said, wresting one of the two rolls from the squirrel-bear-combo-brat. "Are you up to a bit of travel this morning?"

Ahqui's obvious grief at having lost a piece of warm, buttered bread was worthy of an Academy Award.

Matthew caved and returned the roll. If this was what children were like, he wasn't sure he'd be up to the task any time soon.

"Alright. Here you go. Heaven forbid I get a bite to eat."

With a brilliant smile and a truly amazing facility of understanding, Ahqui broke off a crispy piece of the rosungi and offered it to Matthew – (*who took it quickly, before the little beast could change his mind*).

"Erlisherrr?" Ahqui had managed to spit out around a mouthful of food.

"Well... No. Probably not, little cowboy, but we're going to need supplies and I've got somewhere else I've got to go, first."

"I go Matteu. I go."

"You know how to hide, don't you, Ahqui?"

The impossibly cute satellite ears sat up and rotated towards him with comic alertness and Ahqui swallowed what he had been chewing to nod solemnly.

"Good! That's what I needed to hear, little cowboy! 'Cause where we're going, you wouldn't exactly go unnoticed.

Matthew cast his eyes about the katsan for Cynthia or Brisballah, but found neither.

There were a number of cleverly-woven baskets by the door for one purpose or another, and Matthew thought that shoving Ahqui into one of them and draping it with a cover of some sort would provide an adequate hiding place for Ahqui.

What am I going to do about Brizz? He thought, chewing on a tart, blue peach-like thing.

The plan was to get him somewhere safe before heading home, and I've done that, but...

Matthew was fully aware that the chubby Jurrah had already killed once for him, and stood ready to do it again, should the opportunity present itself.

How do you leave that kind of a friend behind? What do you say?

"Sorry old pal, but I can't take you along this time. Just wait here with the Agrigars, and in all probability I'll show up again at some point... blah, blah, blah..."

It wasn't that Brizz couldn't pass as human back home in Maryland, but what if the guy should take it into his head to viciously mutilate somebody all of a sudden?

It had been quite a shock the first time around, and Matthew didn't think it would go over well in Anne Arundel County. They had laws about stuff like that.

It's not as if I'm never coming back. Matthew thought. *Tori and I plan to do a bit of interdimensional sightseeing in the near future, and Alisha still needs finding.*

Matthew swallowed a lump of food and nearly choked getting it down. He mimed a drinking motion for Ahqui and sent him off to fetch a mug of ale.

Brizz would be damn good company on an adventure like that. You never really knew what was going to be waiting for you on the other end of a portal, did you? Ahqui showed up with the ale and Brisballah a few minutes later, bringing an abrupt end to that line of thought.

Matthew still had no idea what he was going to say to the man that wasn't – well – a man at all, strictly speaking.

Made for Breaking

"So, you see, we have quite an unusual predicament, um…" Carolyn looked for the woman's name. "Nurse Cannon. Carolyn finished, diplomatically.

"Margaret is fine, thank you," she smiled without a hint of warmth. "Hm. Yes. I do understand your need to take this baby out of our nursery and down to the Intensive Care Ward," replied the Nurse Cannon. "However, you must know that allowing a new infant to be taken into an area that poses a considerable threat to her health would be extremely unwise."

"But, her mother…" started Carolyn.

"Her mother has not yet regained consciousness, and would not likely be aware of the infant's presence," Nurse Margaret completed Carolyn's sentence with the abruptness of a firmly–closed door.

"But, her grandfather would like to see her! Surely, you can understand how much such a thing could help him to recover from..."

"A myocardial infarction – yes – as I've said, Mrs. Whitley, I do understand your request and I must deny it. No infant will leave this floor for 48 hours. After that, the parents have full authority to take the child wherever they wish, though I'll tell you right now that the ICU does not allow children under the age of 11 to enter that ward – even during visiting hours."

"Well, I have to tell you that I find this situation extremely frustrating," Carolyn said, casting a glance over to Rhamas, who was cradling his daughter close to his chest with an idyllic grin upon his face. "Yes. I can see you are frustrated," the prickly, straight-backed charge nurse replied.

"May I suggest that you photograph the baby for your husband, and, in the meantime, see if you can get his cardiologist to clear him for a visit to our floor?"

"Well, I suppose, if that is our only option."

"It is, I'm afraid." Nurse Cannon turned on her heel.

"I do apologize, Mrs. Whitley, but I am expected elsewhere at the moment, please excuse me."

"Yes. Of course! Thank you. I appreciate all of your

help and advice," Carolyn said, watching the nurse walk away until she was out of sight.

"Rhamas! Good news!" Carolyn chirped, joining Rhamas and her new granddaughter on the other side of the nursery. "We have permission to take her downstairs to see Mr. Whitley!"

"Oh! That is good!" the young man said, beaming. "We will go now."

Carolyn knew that Tori would be along any minute expecting to meet them at the elevator, but – as the saying went – one had to 'go' while the 'getting' was good – and who knew when the charge nurse would come charging back.

She pushed the down arrow authoritatively and waited, never taking her eyes off the corridors to the right or the left of them for any sign of trouble.

What is the harm? Carolyn fumed, internally. *Rules! A lot of hullaballoo over nothing! Of course the baby can go with her father to see her grandfather! Ridiculous! I'm not going to let some sanctimonious, pencil-pushing matron tell me what I will or will not do with my grandchild!*

Still, regardless of Carolyn's constant assurances to

herself, sweat had begun to bead on her upper lip and along her hairline, and she couldn't help feeling as though she was about to rob a bank or commit a murder.

"The small room for going down is here." Rhamas' voice caused Carolyn to jump.

"What? Oh! Yes! Let's go, then, shall we?"

But, as soon as the unassuming group had stepped into the elevator, a deafening alarm had begun to wail throughout the unit, and several nurses, doctors and orderlies had come running towards them – stethoscopes and papers flying.

Carolyn's eyes fell upon the baby's bracelet, and then she knew,

They've encoded it.

"Uh-oh." Carolyn gulped and stepped meekly off of the elevator, motioning for Rhamas to follow with the baby.

The Knowing

There are those who will tell you that being in a comatose state for any length of time makes no lasting impression on one's subconscious mind.

Alisha, who knows differently, is loath to argue the point. She has traveled through alternate realities, learned exotic languages and befriended alien beings. What you believe or don't believe holds little interest for her, as you are childlike and innocent in Alisha's eyes – no matter your age.

The spirit that greets her upon waking is all that's left of her father, and his body has closed itself to him forever. Everything that is Grant Whitley, Esq. is in transition to another place. There is no time for a prolonged visit.

Alisha understands.

A final joining between her spirit and body will probably render her father's spirit invisible, yet she knows that her time away is at an end, and it is time. So, of necessity, the father and his daughter must pass each other only briefly while a thousand words and impressions pass between them, all conveying messages of love and protection.

Alisha smiles weakly around her breathing apparatus, as this is enough.

Forever, and from this day onward, Alisha Lynn Whitley will have the knowing of many things, and there is peace aplenty in this knowledge ...

Look Who's Coming to Dinner

With loyal Brisballah pushing his chair and Ahqui wriggling impatiently in his lap, Matthew Whitley moved steadily towards the big red portal known as the Ghama Traya. There hadn't been any good way to leave Brizz behind – at least, none that Matthew had been able to come up with in the time allotted. He wasn't sure how Maryland was going to feel about his new companions, but Matthew was becoming increasingly unconcerned about anyone's opinion of anything.

Surely, if he needed to pop out of Odenton and back into Natalo I, it would be no big deal. Then, anyone who had a problem would have plenty of time to come to terms with it during his prolonged absence.

Matthew's mind had already expanded beyond the limits of his little car repair and parts business. As much as he enjoyed that kind of thing, he was now on the verge of becoming an interdimensional inventor / explorer / crusader.

There were other vehicles in other worlds that would require his attention (at least, he thought there must be). His mom would be disappointed that he had seen no signs of his sister, but she'd be so happy to have him back home that she'd probably take the odd little Jurrah and stinky squear in stride.

I can probably keep the whole axe-murderer thing under wraps, he thought. *No need to scare anybody. Besides, I'm planning a return trip with Tori, like, soon.*

The thought of seeing Tori again filled Matthew's chest with silver minnows.

Tori.

The rock sat just where they'd left it on the other end of a fallow field.

"Ichsi Ghama Traya gat," Brizz commented in undecipherable Jurrah.

"I see it," Matthew replied – getting the gist. The chair came to a stop within inches of the portal stone before he saw Tori's signal – something very odd sticking up out of the dirt with a – what was that(?) – a purple-colored hair band twisted around the tip?

Tori!

Tori had made it through the portal and left a token for him to find! There could be no other explanation, and he was so proud of her for thinking of it!

"Keesa?"

Seeing Matthew's reaction to the funny stick, Brizz had bent over and plucked it for closer examination, pulling the odd worm-like bit off the end and rolling it between his fingers.

How do I explain this one? Matthew thought. Then, using the hand signs for "my friend," he took the hair tie from the Jurrah and pulled his own hair back.

"Ah," Brizz said in the universal sound for "got it, dude."

Next, Matthew had only to open the OGA (Otherworld Gateway Atlas) to the correct page for the Ghama Traya portal to find the appropriate hand placement for his return to Maryland, and the motley crew was on its way.

Pick-Up Line

Tori put her cell on speaker, dropped it into her cup holder and answered while backing out of the driveway.

"Hello, this is Tori."

"Is that my portal-hopping, world-conquering girlfriend, Tori?"

The shock of hearing Matthew's voice emanating from the cup holder caused Tori to slam on her brakes and ease over to the shoulder – almost causing an accident and earning her a WTF salute from some guy in a silver Audi.

"Are you back?" She asked, seizing the phone and pressing it to her ear.

"Yes, ma'am, I am," Matthew answered with what he thought passed as Southern charm.

"Oh my God! Why didn't you come straight back? Your mom is just about out of her mind with worry."

"Long story," he said, feeling guilty. "Where is

everybody? I came home to an empty house, and nobody's answering their cells?"

Tori put the car in park and sighed heavily. "It's not good, Matthew," she said with a heavy heart.

"Why? What's happened? Is it my mom?"

"No. Your dad had some kind of a heart attack and he is in the hospital. I saw him, and he's – like – talking and stuff. Your mom is there, and – listen to this -- she just told me Alisha is, too."

"What?"

"Look, I'm on the way to the hospital right now. Let me swing by and pick you up, Okay? I know that seeing you will make everything a whole lot better for everybody concerned. I'll explain on the way."

"Wow. Sure. I've got to get cleaned up first, Tori. I'm a wreck," he said with candor.

"I'll bet," she replied with a grin. "Okay. Just hurry. I'll be there in a couple of minutes. Leave the door open and I'll wait."

"Tori?"

"What?"

"I didn't come back alone."

"You… What?"

"I'll introduce you to everyone when you get here."

"Matthew! What have you done, now?"

"I had to bring them," he said, "No worries. I'll tell them you're coming so that they don't, like, hack you into pieces or anything…"

"You'll what?"

"Gotta' go, sweet knees," he said, teasingly. "Man needs a shower and a change of clothes."

"Matthew … what on earth …"

The line went dead and Tori shook her head as she eased the car back onto the road with a sideways grin on her face in spite of herself.

What have I gotten myself into? She wondered.

Facing the Music

For the second time in as many days, Rhamas found himself facing the grim reality of hospital security officers. They looked angry. But, when the head nurse came plowing around the corner towards the 'scene of the crime,' her finger wasn't wagging at him. She was going for Alisha's mother. "I know what you're going to say," Carolyn Whitley started, with both hands facing forward and slightly raised in a posture of surrender. "I shouldn't have attempted to take the baby off this floor."

"No. You shouldn't have," the nurse's arms were crossed and Rhamas could have sworn her cornflower blue eyes were trying to burn new holes into Carolyn's head. "What did you think was going to happen, Mrs. Whitley? Did you think we were just going to let you walk off with one of our babies?"

"Did you just call my granddaughter one of 'your babies?' Tell me you didn't just profess ownership of my daughter's first-born child like some kind of a fairytale witch."

Rhamas took a step backward and was made to think better of that when the guards moved closer to surround him.

Since Rhamas had never seen two such women squaring off before, he felt the need to get himself and his daughter well outside of punching range.

"I think I made myself clear when I explained the hospital policy as it pertains to…" the charge nurse bristled.

"As it pertains to depriving a dying man from seeing his first grandchild?" Carolyn rebutted.

"Oh, come off it. As I explained before, there is no reason why you couldn't have made arrangements for your husband to visit this nursery."

"What is the big deal here?" Carolyn shrugged her shoulders and raised the volume on her protest. "We just want to take her off the ward for a few minutes! What if hearing the baby helps bring my daughter out of her coma? Hmm? What about that?"

"If your daughter becomes well enough to care for the infant, she'll be moved back to our ward and can see the child as often as she wants! For now, however…"

"Bullshit! This baby was due to go home in the morning!"

Carolyn shook her finger and looked so menacing that even the guards turned away. "Her mother needs to see her. Don't you think the mother, father and grandparents have greater authority over where this child goes than you do? Tell me, when did you become the Wicked Witch of the West? Was it during your first year as a candy-striper, or did you become increasingly evil over time?"

This last sentence seemed to echo through the hallways and hang there, like trails of smoke from the back of a burning broomstick. Everyone within earshot found a point on the wall, ceiling or floor to look at, all of them wishing they could be somewhere else. Rhamas was no exception, gulping repeatedly even though everything he swallowed moved like glue.

Then, out of the awkward silence there came a burst of laughter, followed by another until everyone was giggling, chuckling or guffawing to their fullest measure.

Margaret Cannon pulled a pair of surgical scissors

out of her pocket and wasted no time in snipping the baby's bracelet free from her tiny wrist.

"Well, I guess you told me," the nurse laughed, wiping her eyes. "I probably needed to hear it, too!" she added.

"Officer Reynolds, please escort these people to the ICU for me, will you? Make sure they get that child back here in the same condition in which she left."

"Thank you so much." Carolyn burbled, awkwardly. "You can't begin to know how much this means to us."

"I think I've got some idea now, hon. Nobody needs to drop a house on this old girl. Now, get out of here before I change my mind."

Love at First Sight

Brisballah's mouth hadn't closed since the second he set foot in Matthew's front yard. Strange shiny objects zoomed by with people inside, and fancy houses were everywhere – made out of something that looked like colored planks of wood, but wasn't.

Matteu had taken Brisballah by the hand and pulled him into a big house that had things inside to sit on and a shiny wood floor. Brisballah thought it was too big for one family, but didn't say so. Maybe Matteu was son of King or Great Wizard in this world?

The first thing Matteu had done after shutting the door was to pull that same flat black box out of his pocket and push it with his finger until lights and sounds came out of it, then he – this is the strangest part of all – started talking to it! Brisballah even thought he could hear somebody's voice talking back.

Ahqui had gone straight into the room where food was stored and was pulling perfectly-cut pieces of bread out of a see-through bag and shoving them into his mouth with unabashed glee.

Brisballah had spoken sternly to the animal, and picked him up off the floor. Surely it was not a good thing to take the food without first asking permission? He didn't know the proper conduct in this world, but he had to assume that this rule was the same everywhere.

"Brizz? Where are you, dude?" Matteu was calling from another room. "Oh, there you are! Come see this, you're gonna freak out."

Brisballah had no idea what Matteu was talking about, but it was clear that he was supposed to follow, so he did. What he saw next was a very amazing thing! There was water coming out of the wall in a tiny room called a *'shauer'*, and that is where the Maryland people go to wash themselves!

Matteu showed him good-smelling potions and pastes to put on his hair and body and teeth that made a white foam – like from the sea – all over you and made you very clean.

Ahqui already knew about the little room with water, because he went right inside and started rubbing the good-smelling foam all over his body and letting the water rinse it off. Brisballah wondered if they had *shauers* where Ahqui came from, and why nobody had thought of them on Natalo I?

Brisballah stayed in the little room for a very long time. He liked the way the water felt, and the way the smells all mixed up with the smoky water.

When all three of them were washed and dried, Matteu brought Brisballah 'Maryland' clothing to put on. It was very strange with clasps and closings that he had never seen before, but he thought he looked good in the clothes.

Matteu showed him how he looked in a *"meeroar,"* which is a shiny metal that shows your reflection like still water in a pond.

They ate some of the bread with meat -- very flat meat -- and cheese. Matteu called that a "sandwietch." It was very good, whatever it was, and he had been mighty hungry.

The best thing happened when a bell rang for no reason and the door opened. There was a beautiful woman coming inside Matteu's house and she had one of those things for hair pulling all of her hair up like a waterfall from the back side of her head. So pretty, this woman!

Brisballah's chest was pounding hard and his mouth was exceedingly dry.

"Ai. Hai," was all he could think of to say.

The pretty girl said words back, but it was 'Maryland-speak', and he didn't know either end of that.

This was a very strange place, Maryland.

Brisballah hoped there were lots more pretty women here, like Matteu's woman.

With characteristic enthusiasm, Ahqui burst forth from the adjacent room and turned a series of endearing somersaults towards the new arrival before launching his fuzziness fully into her open arms and planting a wet kiss upon both cheeks.

"Oh! I know who you are!" Tori cooed an octave higher than she had ever cooed before. "You are Ahqui, aren't you?"

Just then, Matthew emerged from the hallway looking rosy-cheeked and slightly damp in a fresh pair of jeans and a red tee that proclaimed "I Love Diet Coke!" in broad white letters across the front.

"That's him, in the flesh," Matthew agreed.

"How did you get him? Where ...?" Tori stammered, still clutching the wriggling squear close to her chest.

"That's a long story. Too long for right now, I'm afraid." Matthew wrenched Ahqui free from Tori's grasp and handed him over to Brizz. "Here. Can you keep an eye on him while I'm gone?"

Brizz, catching the gist of his assignment, nodded agreeably.

"Tori Chandler, this is Brisballah I-don't-think-they-have-last-names-over-there. I just call him 'Brizz' for short."

"Brisballah, this is my girlfriend (Matthew paused to get Tori's assent, and got it with a blush) Tori."

"Well? We had better get to the hospital, right?" Matthew asked Tori, expectantly."

"Do you really think it's safe to leave them alone? Here? In your mother's new house, with all her new stuff?"

Brisballah thought that he caught Tori's hesitation and spoke up.

"Brizz watch squear. Keep things good."

Matthew sighed heavily and took Tori aside.

"I have doubts, but there are very few choices available to me under the circumstances, wouldn't you agree?"

Brisballah was trying very hard not to take offense at the pretty woman's lack of trust. He knew that he would earn her trust over time.

"Brisballah is Jurrah Hunstman," Brizz said. "Brisballah will guard house of Matteu. You go. I stay."

Matthew and Tori exchanged one more look and Tori shrugged.

"Okay," she said, reluctantly. "Let's get going."

Reaching Out

Alisha knew that her father was dead, and she was at peace with that knowledge – still, she needed to reach out to tell someone on the nursing staff that she was alive and awake! She wanted to call out, but the life support tubing and wiring had her pretty much mute and immobile for the moment.

With some difficulty, Alisha located the call button on the remote that was dangling awkwardly from her bed rail and pushed it, repeatedly.

"How can we help you?" a distant, yet professional voice asked from everywhere.

"Mm awake!" Alisha tried to get the words past her breathing tube. "Hem mm."

"What? I'm sorry. I can't understand you. I'll ask your nurse to stop in and check on you when she's available."

The speaker crackled off and Alisha was alone again and feeling frustrated.

I guess I'll have to wait until my nurse is 'available,' Alisha thought, angrily.

Where are my parents? Where is Rhamas?

Alisha remembered a movie that she had seen where a comatose patient had awakened after many years to find that everything had changed and her family had long ago given up hope.

What about my baby girl? Is she a grown woman? Have I missed her infancy, toddler and teen years? Alisha's blood pressure monitor began to beep in a frantic rhythm, and alarms of different kinds were set off all around her bed. "What is going on around here? Where is my nurse? Where is my family? Where is my baby?"

Frustrated beyond imagining, Alisha began to pull her breathing and feeding tubes out hand over hand. Once they were free from her throat, they popped out of her mouth trailing a small string of blood-tinged mucus across her lips, chin and the front of her gown.

"Help! I'm awake! My father is dead! I need help! Where is everybody?"

When her cries still went unanswered, Alisha tried the call button again.

"Yes? How can we help you?" the same, measured and pleasant voice poured from the same unseen speakers.

Alisha cleared her throat and prepared to get her point across as clearly and succinctly as possible.

"Hello! I am Alisha Lynn Whitley! I don't know what room I'm in. I think I was in a coma! I am awake now! My father is in here, too! I'm pretty sure he's dead! Please send somebody in here? I need help!"

"Calm down – did you say your name was Alisha? Who is your nurse?"

Alisha threw the call-button remote out of exasperation and rage, but it didn't go very far because it was tightly lassoed to the bed rail.

Distracted Driver

Matthew smelled terrific. Tori had loaded up his chair and they were on their way to the hospital.

Tori was trying her hardest to keep her eyes on the road, but it wasn't easy with Matthew sitting so nearby and looking all squeaky clean and handsome.

"Hey! Keep your eyes on the road over there!" Matthew teased, when he noticed how often her eyes were turning towards him.

"I can't help it! You look great, and smell even better! Can I get a kiss at the next light?"

Wow. Did I really just say that? I think I did! Tori thought, blushing scarlet. She dared a peek in Matthew's direction and found that he was every bit as flushed as she must be.

"I mean... Well... I've really missed you, and I've been worried sick!" Tori knew she was babbling, and wondered how Matthew was taking her sudden lack of restraint. "I can't believe you stayed so long when you really should have come straight home, you know."

Tori was still prattling aimlessly when they pulled up to the next traffic light. Imagine the way her entire body short circuited when she felt Matthew's hand on the back of her head and saw that he was leaning forward for a kiss!

The pleasure that followed was like having unicorns and rainbows dancing around in her private bits and shining out of her ears. Unfortunately, the driver of the red Ford 150 behind them was less amused. The impatient honking of his horn pulled the couple apart in a nano-second and did much to clear the fog in their heads as well.

A few moments of awkward silence followed as Tori made the last turn into the hospital parking garage and switched off the engine. Tori wanted nothing more than to grab Matthew and continue their kissing session, but there was something about a hospital parking garage that put a pall over everything.

"So, my Dad is okay?" Matthew asked.

"I think so. I mean, they were talking about keeping him for a few days, but he was awake and talking and stuff."

"Did my mom say why Alisha was here?"

"No. That was the weird part."

"What do you mean?" Matthew asked, looking worried.

"She asked me to meet them by the elevators on the fourth floor." Tori answered. "She said there was somebody with her that they wanted me to meet."

"Ah. Do you think she brought that guy back with her?"

"You mean Rhamas, her husband?"

"Jeez. I'll never get used to that," Matthew dropped his face into his hands then combed his fingers through his freshly-shampooed hair.

"Yeah. But, why would they come here?" Tori asked as she unbuckled her seat belt and swung open the car door.

"Well, I guess we'll never find out by sitting in the garage," Matthew teased.

"You've got a point there, Whitley. C'mon. I'll get your chair."

"Cool. Thanks," Matthew replied with a laugh.

Ups and Downs

The very second that they moved past the first-floor information desk with pink visitor tags clipped to their clothing, Tori and Matthew ran smack dab into Carolyn, Rhamas, the tiny baby girl and their personal security guard.

"Matthew?" Carolyn cried out in disbelief. "Matthew! Come here and hug me! You found your way back! Oh, Matthew! Now, I just have to get your father and sister on their feet so that I can relax and be truly happy about the baby!"

From his vantage point in his mother's arms, Matthew's head shot up and took in the foreign-looking dude with the bulging muscles and curly hair that was standing nearby with an interested look on his face.

"Rhamas?" he asked everyone within earshot.

The "Field and Stream" model nodded and flashed Matthew a prize-winning smile.

"You are Skink, yes?" Adonis spoke.

That's him, Matthew thought, *the alien guy from another dimension who married my sister.*

"Uh-huh," Matthew replied with his mouth agape.

Then it hit him. The big dude was holding a tiny bundle that looked for all the world like a... No... It couldn't be... It looked like a...

"Did you say there was a -- baby?" Matthew gulped and stared at the parcel in the pink-and-white striped blanket and thought he saw it move. Yes! It was moving...

"Is that a..." Matthew pointed at the wriggling entity just in time to see a tiny hand thrust out and make a fist.

"Baby?" he finished, already knowing the answer.

That's my sister's baby, alright, Matthew thought, entranced. *I recognize the fist.*

Tori squealed and made a fuss over the infant the way he probably should have, but wasn't prepared to.

"Is dad..."

"Yes. He'll be fine. It was an awful shock, but he is handling it well, and he'll probably be released in the next day or two."

Matthew came to the sudden and crushing

realization that he had probably caused his father's illness and it mortified him.

"What happened? Was it my fault for disappearing the way I did?"

"No. Matthew, honestly, I never even had a chance to tell him that you were – gone – to that – place," Carolyn faltered, shooting a meaningful glance at the nosy security guard who was dutifully shadowing the assemblage.

Matthew sucked in a deep breath and sighed with relief.

Whew. It wasn't me. I don't think I would have ever been able to forgive myself if I had caused this.

"So, it was finding out about Alisha that took him down. Was that what happened?"

Rhamas hung his head as this accusation was seemingly leveled at him.

"Alisha needed her father and mother. She was very sick."

Matthew's mom patted Rhamas on the shoulder and spoke quietly.

"He wanted to be here for Alisha, of course. Nobody

is to blame for his illness. Grant's heart has been like a time bomb just waiting to explode for goodness knows how many weeks, months or years. The important thing for us all to remember is that he is going to be okay. Let's just stop placing blame and try to be thankful for that."

Matthew's eyes narrowed. "Where's Alisha, anyway? Can I see her?"

The silence that followed sent a jolt of icy fear the length of his body.

"Mom?"

"She's fighting for her life, Matthew," Mrs. Whitley's voice was barely audible. "We're taking the baby to her now. It will be good for you to be there, too," she wiped her eyes. "Maybe knowing that you are nearby will help to bring her back to us."

"Back to us? What do you mean? She just had a baby, right? That's not such a big deal."

Matthew was losing it.

Tori put her hand on his back and kissed him on the cheek.

"Having a baby can be a big deal. She needs us to be the strong ones. Don't fall apart now, okay? Let's just go give Alisha lots of reasons to go on living." Matthew met his mother's eyes.

"Is it really that bad?" he asked.

His mother nodded and her demeanor was grave.

Matthew had traveled between dimensions, been held captive by Jurrah huntsmen, witnessed two gruesome axe murders and ransacked an evil wizard's abandoned home, but nothing had ever shaken him as badly as the look on his mother's face at that moment.

Alisha can't die. She's a mother, for cripe's sake!

This fervent conviction roared from somewhere deep inside him, but Matthew made no sound as he followed the others to Alisha's room in intensive care.

A Voice from Beyond

"Hello! I am Alisha Lynn Whitley!"

The familiar voice echoed ghost-like from the nurse's station on their right.

"I don't know what room I'm in. I think I was in a coma. I am awake now!"

"Alisha!" Rhamas tucked his daughter against his body and broke into a run, followed shortly thereafter by his security escort who was urging Rhamas to 'slow down' and 'be careful with that baby'.

"That's my daughter, Alisha. She's in 113! Please hurry!" Carolyn made a brief stop at the nurse's station to impart these directives before hurrying off down the hallway towards her daughter's room.

"My father is in here, too!" the tiny voice added. "His name is Grant Whitley. I'm pretty sure he's dead! Please send someone in here. I need help!"

"Dead?"

Carolyn Whitley stopped. Her feet stopped. Her breathing stopped. Her heart stopped.

Dead?

Then Tori Chandler was at Carolyn's side, urging her forward with a rapid-fire stream of encouraging words.

"He probably does look dead to her. Remember how he looked to us when we first saw him under all of that hospital hardware? Remember how pale he was?"

"Come on, Tori urged. "I'm sure everything will be okay. We just have to get in there to sort it all out. Let's go, Mrs. Whitley, you can do this! Only a few more steps and we'll be there. Alisha is awake! She'll be so happy to see you! Think about it! This is wonderful news!"

Matthew, Rhamas and the baby were already out of sight, but the security guard was standing in the hall outside room 113 looking stricken and ill at ease when Carolyn and Tori arrived.

"Dad? Daddy? Dad! Wake up! Dad! It's Matthew!" Carolyn could hear the desperation in her son's voice before she even turned the corner and it struck fear in her heart.

"I'm here, Dad! Wake up! Please wake up! Help!

Nurse! He's not breathing! Somebody! Anybody! Help!"

The code had been called by the time Carolyn reached Grant's side. Lights flashed and white soles squeaked against shiny linoleum as more staff than she'd seen since they'd arrived and rushed in with carts and urgent voices and bade her to "Please step back and let the doctors have some room," but Grant's hand was cold in hers, and his lips were very blue.

Carolyn Whitley already knew it was too late.

Erlisherrr!

A squear (sounds like 'bear') is a bouncy, inquisitive and mischievous creature. It looks like a two-foot-tall teddy bear with the longest, fluffiest, most-personable tail you can wrap your head around.

Ahqui is every bit such a darling, and he knows it – which heightens the caretaker's level of peril considerably! In this instance, he is under the stewardship of a valiant Jurrah huntsman by the name of "Brisballah".

Though Brizz is doing his utmost to contain Ahqui, the little squear has succeeded in exploring every inch of the Whitley household with wildest abandon. Each time the squear is successfully cornered and detained, Ahqui manages an impossible, yet quite well-executed, acrobatic diversion and is off to parts unknown!

Then -- just as Brisballah is ready to give up and allow the animal to have his way – there is a span of dreadful silence.

Gah! Qis e nen menoti wen? Brizz wondered. (Which is Jurrah for – "Uh-oh. What's that little devil up to now?")

Brizz walked the length of the one-level home. He peeked into every doorway, but saw no sign of the troublesome squear – until he turned right at the end of the hall and came upon a touching scene.

The squear was sitting atop a large, wooden box with one of those 'meeroars' on the wall behind it. When Brisballah went closer to see what Ahqui was holding, he saw that it was an image framed in silver of a pretty woman's face.

It looked to Brizz like the human girl who had taught songs to the Jurrah and Agrigar children on Navalo I.

The little one met Brisballah's eyes with his own misty ones and spoke aloud one single word, "Erlisherrr."

That can't be the end...Right?

Hello! This is Kaye Giuliani, author of "The Corn Maze" series. As a reader of anything and everything, I know how devastating it is to finally reach the end of your favorite series.

Readers of the "Charity Fish" trilogy often write to complain that I left them adrift on a sea of "more!" Let me assure you that I will be revisiting both of these series in the future. When you love your characters as much as I do, you can't just leave them dangling out there -- woefully unwritten about -- for any length of time.

Will Alisha and her baby be released from the hospital? What will Alisha and Rhamas name their little girl? How will Carolyn manage her life without Grant at her side? And, what about the budding romance between Matthew and Tori? Will they marry and become inter-dimensional travelers, themselves?

So many questions!

We can all imagine the touching reunion that will surely take place between Alisha and Ahqui. Can we envision Carolyn with a blue tattoo on her face, living happily among the Fendis in Topazial? As an author, I hope to always keep you wanting more! The threads I have left in your hands are just waiting to be woven in your dreams.

If you have enjoyed reading any of my books, please take a few minutes to find me on Amazon.com and leave a review! Just click on the book as though you are going to purchase it, then find the gold stars and follow the links to rate your experience. You can learn more about my latest projects at *www.brigandbooks.com*

I'll finish by saying that I love nothing more than hearing from my readers, so feel free to e-mail me at kayegiuliani@gmail.com!

Thank you for taking this amazing voyage with me.

Kaye Giuliani